D0040868

JE 1 8 20

Raising Lumie

Also by

JOAN BAUER

Raising Lumie

JOAN BAUER

VIKING

VIKING

An imprint of Penguin Random House LLC, New York

First published in the United States of America by Viking,
an imprint of Penguin Random House LLC, 2020

Visit us online at penguinrandomhouse.com

LIBRARY OF CONGRESS CATALOGING-IN-PUBLICATION DATA IS AVAILABLE
ISBN: 9780593113202

Printed in U.S.A.   Set in Fairfield LT

1   3   5   7   9   10   8   6   4   2

This is a work of fiction. Names, characters, places, and incidents either are the product of the author's
imagination or are used fictitiously, and any resemblance to actual persons, living or dead, businesses,
companies, events, or locales is entirely coincidental.

For Evan, always and forever.
With special thanks to Regina Hayes—
my editor and friend.

Raising
Lumie

1

The Puppies

IT'S ALL ABOUT warmth right now.

Warmth.

Wiggling.

And eating.

There are seven of them in this L litter. Some black, some a pale yellow beige.

They stay together, they sleep together, mostly in a heap.

No one would think they are the best of the best.

At least some of them are. Maybe more than some.

They are the same size except for the tiny beige

one. She's the littlest, but she acts like the biggest.

A man, Brian, is watching the puppies on a screen. "Have we weighed that little one?"

"Not yet," says Christine, who works with the puppies. "She eats like you wouldn't believe."

"I can see that." Brian watches the littlest puppy pushing through her brothers and sisters to get to her mother's milk. He laughs as she finds a prime spot and sucks away.

"Something tells me not to worry about you," Brian says to the screen.

"We'll see," says Christine.

A boy, Jordan, age thirteen, has seen his share of newborn puppies. He never gets tired of it. He is taking notes for a presentation he has to give at his leadership training class this summer. Jordan would rather do anything than give an oral report to a room full of humans. But he was chosen.

"It's an honor," his mother keeps telling him.

"I'd rather pay someone to be me for that morning." Jordan's throat feels like he's been chewing sawdust just thinking about it.

He writes,

The littlest one is showing courage.
She can push her way through a crowd already.
She isn't waiting for someone to help her.

Jordan knows this can be good or bad, depending. He writes,

What's good about this—
she knows how to get her needs met.
What could be a problem—she might be too
pushy.

Jordan keeps watching. He comes every day after school to watch the puppies grow.

The puppies open their eyes. Their ears open too. Jordan writes,

What's that like for them?
Now they can see?
Now they can hear?

It's too early to tell much of anything.
Who will make it?

Who won't?

But Jordan likes to see if his hunches are right.

He grins as the puppies crawl, squirm, and bump into each other.

He moves his chair closer to the screen. His eyesight isn't the best.

For now, he can see some.

He can see enough.

2

Olive

Dear Time,

Sometimes you're my friend
And sometimes it feels like you're out to get me.
I don't understand how each day has the same
  twenty-four hours,
But some days go so fast
While others feel like they're a month long.
I don't understand how you yank me into the future
  when I focus on my dreams.
How you pull me back into the past
  when I remember things that are over.

Why do some memories stay so strong
And others disappear like they never meant
anything?
Why does last period in school go so slowly?
Why do I remember the answer to a test question
two days after the test is over?
Why do some people have less time on Earth than
others?
Why do flowers have shorter lives than weeds?
Just this month, would you slow down every hour
so I can stay in my house longer
and be with my friends longer?
You are Time. You can do that—right?
You go on forever.
I want to hold on to forever so badly.

—*Olive Hudson,*
former sixth grader

Dreams adjust.

I learned this lesson early.

I take my sheet of blue paper out of my pocket. Here's what I'd written:

I would like a small dog I can carry around.

I would like a dog who won't run away.

I would like a dog who isn't stupid.

I would like a dog who is already trained because
Maudie can't cope with poop in the house.

Maudie is my big sister. Seriously big—six foot three and a quarter inches to be exact. The tallest female I have ever known personally.

I have more to add. I smooth out the blue paper and write:

I would like a dog who will love me basically
forever.

Forever is a complicated word for me.

I am standing in Mrs. Barnstormer's kitchen facing Hyacinth, the most spoiled dog in New Jersey. Being a companion to Hyacinth is my everyday job, which is helping me save up to afford my own dog someday. Already I've bought a leash, a collar, a water bowl, and two chew toys shaped like gorillas.

You can't just have a dream and expect it to come to

you. You've got to get something you can hold on to that shouts, "This is going to happen!"

I wanted to do a lot more for Hyacinth this last year, but her way of going through life is a living example of that ancient saying, "You can't teach an old dog new tricks." My dad called her "intractable," which means she's not moving unless it's her idea.

I can relate to not wanting to move.

I go to the refrigerator and get her special food—real sirloin steak cut into tiny pieces. Hyacinth is so spoiled, she expects to be hand-fed. She looks at the sirloin I'm waving in front of her mouth. I lower my voice to sound older. "You can do this."

Hyacinth waits.

"Look. Being able to feed yourself is a basic life skill. You'll feel better about everything. You'll have respect." I take a bite of sirloin, which tastes good. Hyacinth growls. I toss the meat in her shiny bowl and say, "The journey of a thousand miles begins with one step."

This is what Maudie put on the poster she made last month when we knew we had to move. Maudie wasn't the first one to say it. The poster shows two girls who look like Maudie and me—one tall, one short—stepping out on a long road, unafraid. My sister is an amazing art-ist. You see something like this, you get totally inspired, until you have to take the first step.

Hyacinth sits there. I rub her neck the way she likes it. "You're going to get a new person to be with you tomor-row. Me and my sister, we've got to—"

A *drip, drip* sound. The faucet in Mrs. Barnstormer's kitchen is leaking. I take a look and reach for Dad's multi-tool that I wear on my belt. I unscrew the handle, unfold the pliers, tighten the ring, and screw the handle back on. The dripping stops.

I like fixing things.

My dad taught me to do this. He's a plumber. Actu-ally, he *was* a plumber.

He died six months ago, which is why I'm living with my big sister. Maudie and I met two weeks before Dad died. We're still kind of new at being sisters.

After Dad died, we had one money problem after another, beginning with Dad's biggest customer going bankrupt and not paying him for an entire year's work.

Maudie had to sell her car.

And then we had to sell the house.

But Maudie got a new job as a graphic designer at an

advertising agency in a place no one has ever heard of—Three Bridges, New Jersey—three hours away.

"It's a good job," she told me, "with excellent benefits and health insurance. It will help us get back on our feet."

I look at the blue paper. Under "I would like a dog who will love me basically forever," I add:

> I would also like to mention that this dream is
> nineteen months late!!

I add the two exclamation marks even though Mrs. Cox, my former sixth-grade English teacher, said that exclamation marks were greatly overused by my generation.

I told her, "I don't really see my generation getting over it," and she burst out laughing.

I bring the concept home:

> One dog.
> One girl.
> Going through life together.
> How hard can this be?

I sign it with my initials—OH!

That's me. Olive Hudson.

I fold the paper and put it back in my pocket. Hya-cinth is watching me.

"Bye, girl. I wish I could have helped you more."

I walk out Mrs. Barnstormer's back door remember-ing what my dad told me.

Life doesn't always work out the way you want or expect, but that doesn't mean it can't be an adventure.

At this moment in time—and that would be June 21, 1:43 p.m.—I have zero adventure in me.

3

The Littlest One

THE PUPPIES GROW fast. It's like watching one of those time-lapse videos where everything is sped up.

At three weeks of age, they tried standing, although they weren't sure what to do with their hind legs.

The littlest puppy has good balance. She was the first of the litter to actually stand and not fall over.

She looked surprised when she did it.

The others tried too, and mostly fell down.

Jordan wrote,

Ha! She's a leader.

The puppies learned to sit and walk around, although

their walking was more like tripping and toppling.

Plus, they squeaked. Over and over they went.

The noises were introduced.

Car horns.

Engines.

Sirens.

Thunder.

Babies crying.

Some of the puppies were surprised when the sounds began. Some weren't.

The littlest one doesn't let anything stop her focus.

Thunder?

She keeps eating.

Sirens? Rumbling trucks? Airplanes taking off?

She keeps playing with every toy in the playroom.

Jordan wrote,

I've never seen a puppy this focused.
But can she get big enough to do the work?

Come on, girl, grow!

4

Memories

"OLIVE!" THAT'S MAUDIE calling me. "What are you doing?"

There is no easy answer to this.

What I'm doing is saying goodbye to the empty house.

What I'm doing is standing in Dad's old room and feeling like I'm leaving him behind.

I haven't been in this room for a while. I picture Dad standing next to me wearing his plumber's work pants with all the pockets and the T-shirt I gave him for his birthday that read:

you flushed WHAT down the toilet?

Like most plumbers, my dad loved a good joke. Don't ever hire a completely serious plumber—that's my advice.

My therapist, Tess, wants me to write these memories down. I will later.

"Olive?" That's Maudie again.

"I'm packing." I put my memory notebook and my HUG A PLUMBER TODAY button in a cardboard box.

She shouts up, "We don't have room for anything else!"

On the box I write, This Day Camp—Intensely Important!!!!!!!!!

This Day Camp sounds like you only go for a day—you don't. You go for a week. It's a camp for kids who are dealing with the death of someone they love.

It was Maudie's idea that I should go. "Here's what you need to know about me," she said. "When I'm not sure what to do, I find somebody who does."

When Maudie came to us, Grandma had been staying with me at our house on Pleasant Street while Dad was in and out of the hospital. Grandma's hip was so bad, she couldn't do stairs—she slept on the couch in our living room. Grandma always told me, "We're a small family, but we make up for it by being fierce." When a red car stopped in front of our house and a seriously tall girl jumped out, I knew.

Grandma looked out the window, and even though every step she took hurt, she pushed her walker to the front door, yanked it open, and hugged and hugged this girl, who kept saying, "I'm sorry I'm late, Grandma. I'm sorry!"

"You're here now," Grandma told her.

Maudie walked over to me and stuck out her hand. "You must be Olive. I'm your big sister."

I looked way, way up at her, and said, "No kidding."

She laughed really hard.

I liked that about her instantly.

"Well," she said, "I always wanted a little sister."

I always wanted a big brother, but that didn't seem like the way to get this relationship started, so I said, "Yeah."

I always knew I had a big sister out there somewhere. Maudie's picture was on Dad's dresser. I knew she had dark hair like me and she was good at art. I knew that Dad was worried about her, but he never said why. I knew that she was Dad's daughter from his first marriage, that her birthday was April 16, and that she was sixteen years older than me.

But where she was when I was growing up—that was a mystery.

Maudie had come because Dad had cancer. The doctors had tried everything to make him well. I held my hope high like it was a balloon filled with helium. Two kids I knew had moms who beat cancer. That happens all the time.

Maudie said to me, "Look, we don't know each other well, but something big is happening and we need to handle it together. Okay?"

"Okay."

I felt her strength take over.

She made a painting of sunflowers reaching toward the sun and put it in Dad's hospital room.

She cut up bright paper in crazy shapes, glued them together on poster board, and stuck that near his bed. Nurses from other floors came in to see it.

She wore long shirts and leggings and scarves with floppy fringe.

She had a knitted hat with a jingle bell that hung down in her face.

She had earrings that danced when she shook her head.

She made the best pizza.

Dad said some people change the molecules of every room they enter.

She brought life to the hospital. I could hear the *click-click* of her boots like she was a soldier marching in to fight a war with colors, paintings, and music.

And she brought her guitar. "You play, right?" she asked me.

"I haven't for a while."

"Get your guitar. We need music!"

It took forever to tune my guitar to Maudie's. She strummed a G. "You know this one?" She started singing Dad's favorite dumb song. I jumped right in—he'd taught me too! We sang together,

> *I've got tears in my ears*
> *From lying on my back*
> *In my bed as I cry over you*

"Faster!" Maudie shouted, and I tried to keep up. *Faster.*

"Like we just sucked helium!" Maudie started singing fast and high.

We were laughing and singing.

Maudie shouted, "Big finish!" Dad used to say this. It meant slow the song down and give it all you've got. I tried to copy her strum as we sang together, with Maudie harmonizing.

We brought our guitars to the hospital and played. Dad couldn't sing with us, but his right foot tapped out the beat so strong and he was laughing. It was so good to hear him laugh!

I was sure Maudie was powerful enough to lift the cancer right off of him.

But she wasn't.

THREE DAYS AFTER Dad's funeral, I was sitting by the front window crying so hard, my stomach hurt. Maudie said to me, "How can we show each other what we're about?" She smiled big. "What if you take me to a place that you care about, that is beautiful to you—and I'll take you to one of mine."

What place would I choose? I made a list.

The bridge I've been riding my bike across since
    I was little
Francine's Excellent Ice Cream Shoppe

The library
Gloria's Pet Store

Lists are great because they can crack open your mind and help you find the best answer. And I had it.

"We're going to the adoption center to see the dogs," I told her.

We stopped at the Dollar Daze; I bought three towels because they always need towels at the center.

The nice guard was there when we arrived. "Welcome back," he said to me. I handed him the towels. "We appreciate it, young lady."

We headed back to see the dogs—every kind, every size. Old dogs, puppies. This is beautiful to me. Beautiful and sad, like we talked about at camp.

Beautiful, because dogs are furry miracles.

Sad, because not every one of these dogs will get adopted.

We played with a terrier named Dora and it was hard to leave her. We got to pat Oscar, a big bear of a dog with dark eyes that told me he knew deep things.

I told Maudie, "I just love being with them. I want to have a ranch so I can have dogs running everywhere."

Maudie looked worried at the idea of dogs running everywhere. "But I only need one," I assured her. I raised my arms and a few dogs began to bark just like that.

She said, "You've got a gift."

"They know I love them. Dad and I used to come here every week."

Then it was Maudie's turn. She took me to a small art museum in the woods called the Dyson Gallery.

"Mrs. Dyson was one of my art teachers. She died a few years ago. Her daughters created this museum in her honor."

There was a picture of Mrs. Dyson and a sign: ALL WELCOME. NO CHARGE.

Instantly, I loved this place. The walls were painted different colors—pale pink, rose, bright white, blue gray. You could tell that everything here was special to this family. "See how each room flows into the next?" Maudie said. We climbed the stairs up to the attic skylight. Sunshine poured in. Big, happy paintings lined the walls. The one I liked best was of a garden in the shade.

"See that touch of red from the flowers near the fence, Olive?"

I nodded.

"The red brings your eye right in. Mrs. Dyson painted that. She taught me to have that touch of red in everything I did."

Maudie smiled bright as we walked through every room. I felt so inspired that Mrs. Dyson's daughters had done this for their mother.

I wondered what I could do for Dad.

I said to Maudie, "I don't think a plumbers museum would get a lot of visitors."

She laughed. "You're right. But keep thinking."

5

Lumie

TODAY THE PUPPIES receive their names.

This is a big moment at the Northeast Guide Dog Center.

Since this is the L litter, every name has to start with L. Donors from around the country sent in suggestions.

Some names are crazy, like Lollapalooza and Lincolnshire.

Brian advised Jordan, "When you think about naming a dog, think about what the name will sound like when you have to shout it."

Lollapalooza is not shoutable.

Christine crosses out Lollapalooza and Lincolnshire.

But gradually the committee chooses six names:

Lightning

Lincoln

Leo

Levi

Lola

Lucy

The littlest one has not been named yet. Jordan hopes it doesn't mean that she won't be able to go to a raiser family. Jordan has raised two puppies with his mom over the last three years.

He knows you have to fully commit.

He also knows the experience is beyond what you can imagine. It is, and he tells everyone this: absolutely worth it!

"And now for our little star." Christine writes Lumina on the whiteboard. "That means 'light.'"

An excellent name—Jordan and Brian are smiling. But can it be better?

Jordan raises his hand. "Can we call her Lumie?"

That's it!

Christine adds Lumie's name to the list.

Jordan doesn't say it—he would love to raise Lumie— but this isn't the year for him.

Back in the playroom, Lumie doesn't know about names and how she'll get to know hers.

She doesn't know how she will learn her name from the other names out there in the world; how she will begin to hear her name said by her raiser; and how, eventually, if she graduates and becomes an official guide dog, she will hear her name said over and over by her blind companion.

These are the last two weeks that Lumie will spend with her mother, brothers, and sisters. She runs and plays with her family like she will do this forever.

Lumie's raiser will be Cara, a high school sophomore who, at this moment, is telling her brother that he'd better puppy-proof his bedroom because that's just how the rules go.

"We all agreed to it as a family," Cara reminds him. "Everything off the floor, Bud. This is a danger zone for a new puppy."

Bad news for Bud, since most everything he owns is on the floor.

"I can't even see the rug," Cara says. "I'm trying to remember—is it green?"

Bud's not sure. He lifts dirty laundry from the corner of his room and looks down. "It's blue," he says.

6

Bye

I'M JUST BACK from seeing Grandma. She's doing so much better in her apartment—she has a nurse to help her, and no stairs to deal with. She's happy that Maudie and I are living together. She said Dad would feel the same way.

"I told you, Roger!" Maudie is on the phone talking to her kind-of fiancé, Roger. *Kind-of* because she doesn't have an engagement ring, and close to every time she talks to him she gets angry or sad, which doesn't seem like a good sign for the future.

"I told you, Roger"—her voice sounds strained—"we're going to work it out. Yes . . . I know . . . but we're going to . . . I think you're not being fair."

What I think is, Maudie needs another fiancé.

My best friend, Becca, and I sit on the floor in the empty living room eating pizza and playing Scrabble. She's winning, but only by three points. Becca is so upset that I'm moving, she's mostly building depressing words on the board.

SAD

BAD

LOSS

She lays down her biggest word yet—MISERY—and gets triple points on the M and the Y.

I use the Y to build YAY—not that I feel that way, but I get twenty-eight points for it.

Becca sniffs and uses the A in YAY to make AARGH.

All I have left is a Z and a Q.

Becca wins.

We eat caramel corn and cupcakes. Becca gives me a card. "I made this for you."

Friends Since Kindergarten
Best Friends Forever!!!

It's got pictures of us at different ages with our arms around each other.

"We have shared big things, Olive."

I nod. In fourth grade, she stayed at my house for a week after her parents got divorced. At Dad's funeral we put flowers on his grave at the same time.

We sit here not talking. Her mom comes to pick her up.

"Always and forever," Becca says, sniffling. I'm sniffling too.

I watch her walk down the front stairs.

I am so sick of being brave.

I hear Maudie upstairs tuning her guitar.

"Hey!" she shouts. "We need a new song."

Not now.

"Come on, Olive!" She walks into the living room with her guitar.

I get mine out of the case, tune the strings to Maudie's guitar.

E-A-D-G-B-E

"Close enough," she says. "Let's try this. I'll sing a line and then you play whatever comes to you as a response."

"I don't get it."

"You will." She strums a C and sings, *I'm sorry that we*

have to go. My turn. Uh . . . I strum a G and sing, *I know.*

Maudie does a four-finger pick on an A minor: *I'm sorry this is hard for you.*

I nod, strum a B-flat, and sing, *I know.*

Maudie: *I wish that I could make it right. . . .*

Me: *I wish that you could too*—I hold the *too* really long and Maudie laughs.

She strums a C/G combination and sings, *I believe in you. I really do.*

I smile and play an A minor to B-flat. *And because that's true . . .*

Maudie plays an F. *I'm betting on you.*

We sing it over and over.

> *I believe in you.*
> *I really do.*
> *And because that's true,*
> *I'm betting on you.*

All through the last night on Pleasant Street, I keep waking up and hearing the melody. I'm awake with the song as the sunrise glows through the window. I remember Dad's crazy lists that he would make before starting something new.

"You've got to remember what you've got," he'd say. "Write it down and check the boxes." He *didn't* mean wallet, phone, or house keys.

I take out my notepad, write:

> Courage—check
> Brainpower—check
> Personality—double check
> Hope—

I'm hopeful about living with Maudie, but not about starting over in a new place.

> Hope—

Well . . .

The most I've got is half a hope. I write ½.

Maybe that's too much hope.

I cross out the ½ and write ⅓.

I walk down the stairs of my house that I've walked down a million times.

I walk through the front door of the only place I've ever lived.

The van is packed—Dad's plumbing van. On the side it reads, CALL JOE HUDSON FOR ALL YOUR PLUMBING NEEDS. I lug his tools from the garage and shove them in the back.

Maudie leans against the van, her eyes closed, phone against her ear.

"I don't agree, Roger. And I think that's not fair. . . . Yes, that's what I said."

I'm nodding because that's exactly what she said, and having met Roger, I'm sure she's right—what he said wasn't fair.

Roger came to Dad's funeral and I don't think he comforted Maudie one bit. All he kept saying was, "We need to talk."

Once that day he said to me, "So, who are you going to live with?"

Things hadn't been decided yet and I told him that.

He looked at me with his cold blue eyes. "Just make sure it's a person who really wants you—otherwise you'll have a very unhappy life." He walked away.

I never told anyone what he said, but I wrote it in my journal with the date and time. I wrote some of the wonderful things people said too.

> Your dad was a man of honor.
> Your dad always helped people.
> He never looked the other way.

Later that day, my cousin, Gina, asked, "How does it feel to be an orphan?"

I didn't answer her; I couldn't. Aunt Ceil, Gina's mom, was at the funeral too. She was my mom's older sister. Dad and Aunt Ceil never got along. He once told me, "Aunt Ceil thought your mother should have married a doctor, not a plumber."

I won't be missing her or Gina!

Maudie's in the van now, not smiling. I climb in.

"You ready?" she asks.

I shrug.

She's bad at driving a stick shift. The engine shrieks as she strips the gears.

"Push the clutch pedal all the way to the floor," I tell her.

Maudie does that.

"Now let it out gently and give it some gas."

"How do you know this?"

"Dad taught me."

"Did he let you drive the van?"

"No. He just wanted me to know how stuff works."

"I do what next?" she half shouts.

Olive, pay attention. Once the clutch engages, then you can accelerate.

I tell Maudie this. She tries. "It should be smoother," I say.

Maudie grips the wheel. "Let's stop talking."

"Okay."

"Do you need to have the last word?"

"No," I say.

7

Necessary Parts

MAUDIE ISN'T TALKING. I'm sleeping a little and waking up when she changes gears.

Trees. That's what I see. Lots of trees.

This tells me nothing about where we're going to live.

Maudie's phone rings. It's Roger. She answers on her earbuds. She's listening now . . . for a long time . . . like Roger is giving a speech.

"I'm not sure," she says. "I think we should take a break. . . . Yes. . . . That's what I said." She listens some more. It would be easier if she just put him on speaker so I didn't have to guess. She says, "Well, if that's the way you feel . . ."

This could mean a dozen things.

"I don't look at it that way, Roger."

I think it's nice of her to say that. Maudie is a kind person. He should appreciate that about her.

I think the call is over. Maybe, hopefully, the whole relationship.

Maudie says, "You know, he makes me stark-raving crazy!"

I nod.

"Avoid all guys who need serious adulting, Olive."

I nod again, although I'm not sure what this means.

More driving. More trees.

Suddenly my chest gets tight.

My heart races.

I feel dizzy.

My breath comes in short gasps.

I can breathe, I know I can breathe. . . .

"Olive?"

"I need to get out of the van!"

Maudie pulls over. I jump out and kneel by the side of the road.

It will pass. That's what Tess says. "Panic attacks feel like they'll last forever, but they won't," she always tells me.

I cup my mouth with my hands and breathe in and out. In and out.

I don't remember why this helps, but it does.

"Olive . . . ?" Maudie kneels next to me.

"I'm fine."

"Convince me."

I look at her—she's tired, but so pretty. I take a deep breath, let it out slow.

My breath starts to feel normal again.

"We're going to figure out what you need," Maudie says. "I promise."

"I need a dog."

"Oh, Olive, we can't right now. You know that!"

"A small dog," I say.

"We've talked about this! We need to focus on one transition at a time."

"A dog isn't a transition; it's a necessary part of life."

Two people on bikes stop to check on us. "Are you all right?" the man asks.

Maudie says yes. "Thank you for stopping."

They wait, which is nice. "You're sure?"

I get up so I won't look so helpless.

They wave and ride off.

We walk to the van. CALL JOE HUDSON FOR ALL YOUR PLUMBING NEEDS. I put my hand on the JOE HUDSON and try not to cry.

My mom died when I was two years old. She was in a car accident. I don't remember her at all—I was too little. But I miss her all the same.

For years I hung a secret sign over my life:

Dad will always be here. No matter what.

Now it's . . .

Maudie will always be here. She has to be.

• • •

WELCOME TO THREE BRIDGES,
NEW JERSEY
WE'RE GLAD YOU'RE HERE

Maudie smiles at the sign.

I don't. I look out the window at nothing.

Welcome to my new nothing life. Through the trees, I think I see dogs being walked by a lady.

Maudie turns a corner. I ask her, "Did you see those dogs?"

"No."

"They were wearing green vests, I think." I look behind me. Trees. No dogs.

"Vests?"

"They were all the same kind of dog."

"I think you were dreaming, and I think we're here . . . maybe. . . ." Maudie turns down a dirt road. Another turn and we are now on a side street driving near some houses that all look alike.

She pulls to the side of the road to check the directions.

"Plumber!" A lady shouts it. She is running down the street waving her arms, running right toward our van. "Plumber!"

Maudie and I look at each other. We're in Dad's plumbing van, but . . .

"Plumber!" The lady runs right alongside us, desperate. "The plumber I called two hours ago has not shown up and my kitchen is a mess. I need help now!"

"We're not plumbers," Maudie says. "This is our dad's van."

"Where is your father?"

I'm not sure this lady can handle the news, so I say, "My dad taught me a little about plumbing."

"Well, you're better than nothing," the lady says. "Please, help me."

I get out of the van as Maudie says, "Olive."

I walk to the back of the van and find Dad's plumbing toolbox as Maudie follows me saying, "Olive." She pulls me aside. "We're not going into a woman's house we don't know."

"Plumbers do that all the time," I tell her.

"You're not a plumber."

"Hurry!" the woman shouts. Just then a police car drives by. I wave it down.

The woman police officer stops. I explain. Then I ask, "I'm not supposed to go into houses of people I don't know. Will you come in with me?"

She studies me, probably to see if I'm dangerous. I try to look normal. "How old are you?" she asks.

I lower my voice to sound mature. "Twelve." She looks at me strangely. I add, "But I'm old for my age."

"Hurry!" That's the lady who needs me.

The officer gets out of the police car and walks toward

the house with her hand on her gun. Maudie walks with her. I run into the lady's kitchen. The faucet is spraying out water everywhere. This is one mess of a place.

"Did you try to turn the water off?" I ask.

"I . . . I don't know how to do that."

I don't mention that this is something everyone should know how to do.

"Here. I'll show you." I kneel down and open the door under the sink, shine Dad's flashlight inside. There it is. "See, ma'am, right here is the shutoff valve. You pull it down." The water stops.

"Well, look at that," the lady says.

"It's not fixed yet." The faucet is old and rusty. "You're going to need a new faucet and some new pipe."

"You know how to do that?"

"I do, but I don't have a new faucet for you. I wish I could help more."

"You helped plenty," she says, and offers me twenty dollars.

"Thank you, ma'am—it's free today." I see a small notepad and a pen on the counter. "Could I write something and put it under your sink?"

She nods. I write,

This repair is in honor of Joe Hudson,
the best plumber in America.

I signed my initials like I always do . . . OH!

I look up at Maudie, who is smiling at me.

I stick the note by the shutoff valve and wipe my hands on my jeans. I swear, I feel taller than my sister right now.

As we walk out the door the police officer and Maudie are talking about how we're moving here. The officer says, "We're glad to have women like you in town."

I do a little dance out to the car. I love being called a woman.

The officer climbs in her patrol car, waves, and heads off down the street. Maudie looks at me. "That was impressive."

I shrug and look down, smiling. It was, kind of.

"It was also a perfect way to honor Dad."

I know!

"But one piece of advice, Olive . . ."

"What?"

She laughs. "Next time, take the money."

8

It's Small

"HERE WE ARE." Maudie points at another sign.

> THE STAY AWHILE
>
> OF
>
> THREE BRIDGES, NEW JERSEY

I see a big house, faded yellow with a wraparound porch and vines along the side. It faces a forest of trees.

The van jolts to a stop. An old man on the porch looks up from his newspaper.

"It's a house share," Maudie says.

"What's a house share?"

"Pretty much what it sounds like."

"We share a house with someone."

"Several someones."

You should have told me about this! "What do we share?"

"The kitchen, the bathroom, the living room, the dining room, the porch."

This is not sounding good. "Is there anything we don't have to share?"

Maudie gets out of the van. "Yes. We get two rooms and a closet. It's like going to college."

"I'm not ready for college!"

"But now you will be."

We go from a small house with a million memories to a big place with none!

There's a strange motion on the porch.

Was that a rabbit?

Did I just see a rabbit run into the house?

We walk up to the porch. The old man doesn't look up from his newspaper. "You like rabbits?"

"Absolutely," Maudie says.

"Be careful of the one in the hall." He puts down his paper and shouts toward the front door. "Bunster, be nice!"

I look at Maudie. The old man doesn't smile. "You're on the second floor or third?"

Maudie says, "Second. I'm Maudie, by the way, and this is my sister Olive."

I wave.

The old man sniffs. "Lester Burbank. Lu Lu and Miss Nyla are inside."

We walk inside. All I see is the rabbit sitting on a round rug, looking at me.

"You must be the rabbit in the hall," I say to it, feeling a little like Alice in Wonderland. The rabbit hops off.

Something smells good. I follow the smell to an enormous kitchen. A lady wearing a bright green and yellow head-wrap is taking muffins out of the oven.

"Oh," she says, smiling, "you must be Olive."

"Yes, ma'am."

"I'm Lu Lu Pierce, owner of this rambling old place."

From the hall I hear a woman's voice shout, "Part owner!"

Lu Lu Pierce laughs. Her head-wrap is tied in wonderful knots and folds. I can't help but look at it. "Do you like it?" she asks.

"I love it!"

"It's a dhuku from Zimbabwe. It belonged to my mother. I wear it for special occasions." She smiles at me like I'm extra special.

Another woman walks over and Lu Lu Pierce says, "This is my—"

"I can announce myself. I'm Nyla Pierce, this woman's younger sister." Nyla Pierce isn't wearing a dhuku.

"*Older* sister," Lu Lu Pierce insists. She puts six muffins in a basket and hands them to me. "Normally I make these for breakfast, but they're gone fast. This is my welcome to you."

"Our welcome."

"Thank you. Both."

"Your apartment, 2B, is at the top of the stairs. Sometimes the door sticks."

I smile. The rabbit hops through the kitchen.

This is some kind of place.

THE DOOR STICKS.

Maudie puts her shoulder to it and pushes it open.

I gulp. "It's small." 2B is way too small.

Maudie doesn't seem to mind. "Yes, it is, but everything else around here is big. Remember that. Big porch, big kitchen, big living room, dining room. It's a house share. The only thing we don't share are these two rooms."

I groan. "There's not much space for anything."

"We're going to have to be creative!" Maudie shouts, walking between our two little rooms like a general giving orders, which, I guess, makes me the soldier. "Take this down, Olive."

I sigh.

"We need a huge mirror because that will make this room look so much bigger." I write that down. She raises her hands to the ceiling. "We're going to use the vertical space."

I don't know what this means.

"We need, in no particular order—folding screens and fun colors—seriously fun—but they have to be light. I wonder if Lu Lu will let me paint clouds on the ceiling. We'll need a bold rug and a garment rack to hang up clothes. We'll use our table for the microwave and the slow cooker, and we'll need under-bed storage with wheels. We should have the beds in the same room so that we can have a sitting room—and we'll need a plant. . . ."

"Why do we need a plant?" I could have said that nicer.

"Because it's a living thing that will make us feel happy," Maudie snaps. "Anything else?"

I raise my hand.

"Olive . . ."

"A dog is a living thing that will make us feel a lot more happy than some plant that—"

Maudie's hand goes up. "Enough."

I feel like I'm on some reality TV show where people fix your house up in twenty-four hours and they don't ask your opinion on anything.

"Curtains for privacy," Maudie continues. "Open storage bins." She pauses so the ideas can catch up with her. "I think the bigger room should be for music and reading and art, so we can use the table we already have, but most of what we have is too big. You're with me?"

"Sort of." All I see are two small rooms, and all I can think is, I hate this place. I can't live here.

"We can put baskets on the walls for towels and clothes." Maudie stands there like she can see the whole thing already finished.

I raise my hand, don't get called on.

I can't live here!

Maudie gets out some art supplies, stiff paper, and wets a paintbrush. She draws, using every rainbow color:

LIVE LARGE

"This is what we're going to do." Maudie hangs it in

front of the closet. "We're in a small place, but we're not going to live small."

"Do you actually like it here?" I whisper.

It's like some of the air holding Maudie up gets released. She sits down. "Not yet, but we can make this little place beautiful." She sighs. "And I need beauty."

I look at her face. Her eyes are bright and she's smiling, not a clenched kind of smile, a real one.

"Here's how I'm thinking about it. No bill collectors. A real chance at reducing debt quickly because our rent here is low. I just want to get on my feet, take care of you, do a good job at work, and start saving. I don't want to jump every time the phone rings. I guess I'm relieved. And like the sign says, it's just for a while."

This seems like a good moment for sisters to hug, but Maudie isn't always a hugger—I don't know why.

9

Live Large

WHEN I WAKE up in the morning, the LIVE LARGE sign has more to it—a funny cartoon bird is sitting on the G, and a rising sun is in the background.

I smile. Maudie's been at work.

She's sure not working now. She's sleeping. Maudie sleeps hard.

I walk into our sitting room. She's arranged some of our furniture to fit. I didn't hear her do any of this last night. I'm a pretty good sleeper too. It would be nice to have a LIVE LARGE sign in here. Maybe I could get a pocket-sized one to carry around. I stand by the closet, feeling small.

"The closet will always be a challenge," Maudie says from under the covers. "But we will prevail."

"Okay!" I shout. "Where should the dog live?"

I thought that was a cute joke, but all I hear is an irritated sound from under the covers. "Sorry," I say, "joke flag . . ." Dad and I used to say that. I wave a pretend flag, but her eyes are closed.

This kind of apology doesn't work if the other person is sleeping.

MAUDIE'S ALARM GOES OFF, and my job is to not let her hit the snooze button for eight more minutes. To do this, I slide across the room in my socks to the table between our beds shouting, "No!" and rip the alarm clock from her hand.

"Was that necessary?" she asks.

"You said it was my job."

"You don't have to be so good at your job."

I've already planned my whole day. I'm going to unpack for one hour. Then I'm going to sit out on the porch and read. Unpack for another hour and then call Becca and—

Maudie is checking her phone. "Oh, that's nice." She

looks up. "My boss says you can come with me for the first day."

"Uh . . . I don't want to do that."

"He's a nice guy. It's that kind of company."

She's reading her messages.

"What would I do there?"

"He says there're things for a kid your age."

"Like what?"

She looks up and makes a face. I mention I have to unpack.

"You know what? We don't know the dynamic here yet, so why don't you come with me?"

"I don't want to."

"It's not about wanting to; it's about doing what's smart right now."

"I'm tired," I say.

"I get that, but I'm pulling rank." That means I have to do what she says, like I'm a private in the army.

"Olive, look—"

"I need to be quiet today, Maudie. I promise I won't get lost in the woods."

"Tomorrow you can be quiet. Today, please, drop the foul mood, pull up your adorable self, and come and meet my boss, who is extending himself for you so that you will feel comfortable in this new place. And if you can't do it for him, then I want you to do it for me, and if you can't do it for me . . ."

"Okay!" I walk slowly to the bathroom that we share with a person yet unknown, who is currently in the bathroom.

I wait in the hall. Bunster hops by.

I ask him, "How are you? How's the day treating you so far?"

Bunster looks at me like he might actually answer, but he hops down the stairs, which is pretty funny to watch a rabbit do from behind.

The bathroom door opens; an old lady walks out. She looks at me and says, "Oh, you're the girl."

I nod. I hear the toilet bowl running, which it's not supposed to do.

"It always does that," she says, and walks to apartment 2C, opens her door that doesn't stick, and shuts it tight.

I go into the bathroom, lift the back of the toilet, and use the multi-tool to reconnect the plunger.

No more noise.

The lady in 2C opens her door and looks at the bathroom.

"I fixed it," I tell her. "I do stuff like that."

• • •

IT TAKES ELEVEN MINUTES to drive to Maudie's new job. She pulls into the parking lot. The sign says GOODWORKS.

It's a nice sign, but Maudie could make it better. All I know about this place is that it's a different kind of advertising agency.

"This is going to be great." Maudie's got her game face on.

I groan.

"Okay, sunshine, let's go."

I cross my arms tight and look at my lap, which is non-interesting. My book bag is at my feet. I brought my journal, which I have hardly written in since Dad died. I get it out. "I have to do one thing."

I turn to a blank page and write,

Olive Hudson, orphan.
Olive Hudson, the new girl in town who has no
    friends.
Olive Hudson, the girl who would give anything
    to get her old life back.

I shut the journal. Tess told me to write down what I'm feeling. I can't wait for our video call on Wednesday.

Maudie asks, "Are you ready?"

I look down. "I've got a stomachache."

"For real?"

"Maybe it's more like an overall ache."

"Movement can help with that."

"My mouth feels dry."

"Olive."

"And I think I'm getting a rash." I scratch my ankle.

She studies my face. "Will you trust me?"

This is a hard question, because Maudie has changed her life around to help me and I appreciate that; I just don't want to meet anyone new today, or possibly, ever.

"Will you trust me, Olive, that if for one minute I thought this was a bad idea, I wouldn't ask you to come, even though Brian is my boss, a nice guy, and I want to make a good impression?"

"How long do I have to be here?"

She shrugs. "Half a day."

"What is there to do here for an entire half day?"

10

Ohhhhhhhh!!

BRIGHT COLORS EVERYWHERE. People sit at black desks with short white walls around them. There are flowers on a big round table, and cinnamon buns.

"Take one," a smiling lady says to me.

Everyone is saying hi and welcome to Maudie and me.

I take the second biggest cinnamon bun and feel out of place. I'm about to take a bite when a tall man wearing jeans and a white shirt with the sleeves rolled up walks over. "You must be Olive," he says.

"Yessir."

"I'm Brian. Is it true what I hear?"

"I . . . don't know. . . ."

"I hear you like dogs."

This is a vast understatement, but I'm standing straighter. "Totally. I'm a maniac." Maybe I should have used a different word.

He puts his hands on his hips. "Would you like to meet the puppies?"

My breath catches in my throat. "You have puppies here?"

"Three right now."

"I really want to see them." I gulp down the cinnamon bun, which is so good.

I look at Maudie, who looks back at me like I should have trusted her. There is a word puzzle game on a magnetic wall. One sentence stands out:

if it's already good, can it be better?????

We walk down a hall with more bright colors and posters on the orange wall. Brian stops at a blue door, opens it. There is a low gate there with three small black noses poking through.

"Ohhhhhhhhhhhhhhhhh!" I say.

I look down at the three puppies.

A boy around my age walks over, picks up the puppies, and puts them in a little wagon.

I can hardly stand this intense cuteness, so I say, "Ohhhhhhhhhhhhhhhhh!" again.

"That's what everybody says," the boy tells me.

The littlest puppy is squeaking to get out of the wagon. She's the lightest beige yellow. She shakes her little head and looks at me like, Do something! Help me!

I get on my knees by the wagon. Brian says, "You can pick her up."

Gently but firmly, I lift up this wiggling puppy, who is possibly the most adorable dog in North America.

"Olive," says Brian, "this is Lumie."

I put my nose close to her head and she licks my face. I'm laughing. "Hi, Lumie." And it's crazy—there's part of me that wants to start crying, but that would be unprofessional. I want to show that I can be trusted in every dog situation.

I didn't know there were going to be dog situations here!

I sniff, which I don't think is giving anything away. Lumie is wiggling like you wouldn't believe and her little tail is wagging and we are having a moment, I'm telling you—a major human/puppy moment.

She is scratching my arm just a little. She's like a little fur machine that is 150 percent ON.

"Good girl," I say. "You're a very good girl."

"Wow, she likes you," Brian says.

Of course she likes me!

Now the other two puppies, a little black one and one a little darker than Lumie, want to play too. The boy lifts each one out of the wagon and puts them on the floor. They head for my lap and are crawling all over each other because I'm the new smell in town.

The boy says, "The black lab is Leo, the golden girl is Lightning, and I'm Jordan, the eighth-grade human. Nice to meet you, Olive."

I'm laughing now because Leo is licking my toes that are out there in public due to my flip-flops. Lightning plays with her paws, leaps on Lumie, and they both squeak.

I stand up, but Lumie wants me to hold her. Lightning and Leo jump on my legs. I sit cross-legged on the rug and instantly I am buried in puppies.

I'm never leaving this room.

Leo nuzzles my hand. Lumie paws my arm.

Hi.

Good dog.

Yes, you're a good dog too.

And you. No. I haven't forgotten you!

There are toys all around and different levels for the puppies to crawl on. Now I notice sounds in the room— thunder, rain, horns honking, vacuum cleaners. This is weird.

"We're acclimating them to sounds they'll hear out in the world," Brian explains. "They have to be able to stay focused and calm in any situation to eventually become guide dogs."

"You mean for blind people?"

"That's right. The Northeast Guide Dog Center is an hour away. I do some training for them."

Jordan laughs. "He does a lot more than that."

Brian shrugs. "A few of our GDC employees work with the dogs and we let some of the puppies come here to get socialized."

Lumie climbs into my lap. I put her across my chest and rub her. "Hey, baby. You're too cute."

"You're very good with them," Brian says.

I can totally stay here for half a day. Maybe all week. I

look at Maudie, who is smiling bigger than I've ever seen her. She mouths, I told you.

If you'd told me there were puppies, I wouldn't have been such a pain!

"So, the job here, Olive, is to help the puppies try new things."

I laugh as one licks my toes. "Toes are new things?"

"Your toes are," Brian says. "See if you can get Lumie to go through the little tunnel. She's having a bit of trouble with that."

I stand by the blue tunnel, which is maybe two feet long. I put Lumie in front of it. She runs off then comes back.

"Lumie, come on." I see her wanting to go, but not sure. What's it like to be a puppy with so much energy? Humans stand over you, pick you up, and put you places you don't always want to go.

"Lumie," I say. "This is a good thing."

I give her a gentle push; she shakes her head. "Just try it," I say. "It's fun. This whole room has got fun stuff."

Lumie shakes her head again like a little pony and runs over to Leo. Together they pull a black ring across the floor. I wait till she's done with that, and use a hand motion to get her attention. "Lumie, come."

"She's too little to obey that," Brian says, "but you're smart to get her used to the command."

"Come, Lumie." She bounds over. "Good dog. Go through the tunnel." She pauses. I get on my hands and knees and look at her. "It's just your size." This time, Lumie goes through it and likes it so much, she goes through it again.

"Good dog!" I rub her.

"Nice work," Brian says. "You're probably really busy having just moved here, but if you ever have any free time and would like to help with the puppies—"

"All I have is free time," I assure him.

"These are very special dogs, and we do everything we can to get them ready to become guide dogs for blind people. We teach them to be good citizens—how to behave in a house and out in the world. Where and when to poop. Every step is important."

I ask, "How much hugging does a guide puppy need?"

Brian thinks about that. "I'm not sure we've measured hugging time exactly. One of the goals here is to show the dog that humans are awesome."

I get that, but I hope he's got an answer for me.

Brian smiles. "I can't give you an exact right amount of hugging time, but I've raised eight puppies, and I would say, without question, the answer is—a lot."

I write that down. Put stars around it.

I'm totally serious about working with these dogs.

11

All In

THE BOOK BRIAN gave me about the Northeast Guide Dog Center is amazing. I can't imagine anything better to do with your time than be a volunteer. Being the all-in kind of person that I am, I want to do everything.

First, be a puppy raiser.

Then, be a trainer.

Then, be a supervisor.

Then, possibly, be the president, as long as I can have four puppies in my office at all times.

I haven't been able to talk to Maudie because she's been on the phone with Roger. I can hear her in the sitting room saying, "I don't know what to tell you. I don't have the answer to those questions. . . ."

Among the long and growing list of questions I have is, why Maudie doesn't tell Roger to take a flying leap?

To begin with, they have nothing in common. My dad, when he was trying to make a point, wrote the word nothing as No Thing.

Roger looks like an actor. He is always brushing off his pants. Not a dog person. He knows a lot about wine, he drives a red car, and he has a fake laugh.

He works at a big bank and is always traveling to places like London and Singapore, where there are other big banks. Also, and this is major, Roger doesn't like me. Dad didn't raise me thinking I'm the center of the universe, but I don't like being completely ignored.

Of course, I don't like Roger, either. Maybe, like a dog, he senses that. Actually, if he were more like a dog, I'm sure I would like him.

I'm not even sure Maudie likes him. Her face gets red and splotchy when they talk—and these days they mostly fight.

I think Roger's bank should send him to Saturn.

Back to puppy raising.

I write down my questions.

What would make Lumie not get in the program?
What extra training might Lumie need?
Where do I go to get trained?
How do I convince Maudie this is a good idea?

And here's the Big Impossible I've been reading about that all raisers have to face:

How do you say goodbye to a dog
   you've raised for over a year?
Could I do that?

CRASH!

I hear noises in the hall. Men are shouting.

"What was that?" Maudie runs out to see. I follow her.

A big piece of broken pipe is on the rug in the hall. Some water is on the floor. Mr. Burbank is looking up at a hole in the ceiling. A man standing on a ladder looks down at him.

"It's still leaking," Mr. Burbank says.

"Thank you, sir. I'm aware of that."

"This isn't good," Mr. Burbank says.

"Yeah, we've figured that out."

The man on the ladder is wearing a T-shirt with the words PREMIER PLUMBING. I look at the pipe on the floor. Another man in a PREMIER PLUMBING shirt walks up the stairs carrying a piece of pipe. I can hear Dad say, "If you don't have the right kind of pipe, you can't do the job right."

I raise my hand, clear my throat. The man on the ladder says, "Can we help you?"

I smile. Actually, I can help you. "I think you're using the wrong pipe, sir."

"No kidding . . ." This guy starts laughing at me.

"Yes, sir. My dad's a plumber and he said that aluminum pipe won't do the job."

The guy says, "Tell you what—go do your homework or something—we'll take care of business here."

Maudie stands next to me and stares at this guy. "Olive, what else did Dad tell you that you'd like to share?"

"He said aluminum is cheap and you can never build something that lasts with something that's cheap. You should use copper."

The guy laughs again. "Gee, thanks, kid. I've been at this a long time. Send your father over and we can have a talk."

You have no idea how I wish I could do that.

"How old are you?"

"Twelve, but I'm old for my age."

I look up "copper pipe" on my phone. Yes—it is the best pipe to use. I show this to the plumbers and to Maudie.

The plumber on the ladder says, "Mind your own business, kid. You've got an irritating way about you."

Maudie steps forward. "Excuse me?"

Bunster is watching. Mr. Burbank points to the angry plumber. "Show some respect, because the way you're acting, the chances of you being here for five more minutes are slim."

I reach down to pat Bunster, but he hops away. Lu Lu Pierce walks up and Mr. Burbank says, "I think Olive's got the solution."

I tell her about the copper.

She stares at the hole in her ceiling. "Is this true?"

"I know what I'm doing," says the angry plumber, while the other one says the plumbing supply store is open for another hour and he'll be right back.

Maudie, Lu Lu Pierce, and Mr. Burbank look at me like I'm close to a genius.

This seems like a good time to go back into the apartment before I do anything stupid and change their minds.

12

The Big Impossible

THE NEXT DAY at goodWorks I get to know Christine, who is a manager and a puppy raiser. Plus, she leads tours.

So I ask her the Big Impossible.

"How do you say goodbye to a dog you've raised?'

Christine sits with me. "I've raised five puppies, and when you work with these kinds of dogs, you keep telling yourself, 'This dog is going to change a life.'"

I write down,

THIS DOG IS GOING TO CHANGE A LIFE!!!!!

I'm in the puppy playroom now with Jordan, eighth-grade human, who is carrying Leo, who is wiggling and nuzzling him.

"You've got a dream job, Jordan."

"Yeah, and they don't even pay me."

He puts Leo down and gives him a treat, but he walks close to the puppy and only lets him go so far into the room.

"Nope," he says, picking Leo up and putting him down. "Back to me." He looks at Leo, who looks at him. "That's right. Look to me. Good boy." Jordan picks the puppy up again and puts him over his shoulder. "I did all that, Olive, to teach him to look to one person. He's got to learn to do that with a blind person."

I write that down too. "How come?"

"Because the dogs need to focus. They can't be distracted. They've got to know what it means to work and to be loyal."

I never once thought about that.

I look to the corner of the playroom, where Lumie is sleeping. Puppies in general are all adorable, but she's the one for me.

Jordan says, "You know that Lumie has been assigned to a raiser?"

My breath catches in my throat.

"She's a high school girl, Olive. I just found out about it. She's going to pick Lumie up in a few days."

I thought—well, it was colossally stupid what I thought!

I'm going to need to run out of this room now.

Jordan says, "But there are lots of other puppies, you know, and that's the thing about doing this—"

I don't want to hear any more.

I say, "I'll be right back," like everything is fine, except, if he sees the tears running down my cheeks, he'll know it's not.

Out the door; I race down the hall to the bathroom, run into the last stall, lock it tight. I cover my face and cry . . . quietly.

Inside I'm screaming.

DIDN'T BRIAN KNOW?

"Olive? Are you all right?" This sounds like Christine.

I'm still in the stall. "Yes. I'm fine."

"Listen, Jordan said there might have been a misunderstanding."

No. I understand perfectly.

"It would help if you could come out." This is definitely Christine.

I blow my nose in misery. Dry my face with TP.

Smile.

Walk out, looking down, mostly.

I wash my hands, dry them.

"Can we talk about this?" Christine asks. If she weren't so nice, I'd scream, No!

"I guess."

"Do you want to get ice cream?"

CHRISTINE HAS PEPPERMINT candy crunch and I have rocky road, which pretty much describes my life right now.

She says, "Normally, puppies are matched with raisers. The people at the center usually do that."

"Not Brian?"

"No."

"I thought he did everything." I get a spoonful of chocolate ice cream, nuts, and marshmallow.

"He almost does."

I try to explain. "Lumie and I—we just—"

"I know. It's easy to fall in love with them."

Lumie fell in love with me too!

How do I tell her?

I need this so much!

Christine is studying my face. I'm trying to look

mature and responsible, but I know what she's thinking.

"You're thinking, if I can't say goodbye to a puppy I just met, how am I going to do it with one I raised for over a year. Right?"

"Not right."

"Oh . . ."

She finishes her peppermint crunch and leans back. "I'm thinking that you've got the heart and the dedication to do this. You won't let hurt and heartbreak stop you."

I sit a little taller, pierce a fat piece of marshmallow. "You're right."

"I'm thinking you've got puppy raiser written all over you."

I check my arms. "I do!"

"Okay then, Olive. This is part of it."

"Okay," I say. "Who's the high school girl who's going to raise Lumie?"

"I don't know anything about her. But, Olive, you are now part of Lumie's story. And you always will be."

TESS'S FACE COMES up on video. It's so good to see her. Not sitting in her office on the blue couch, not seeing her in her swivel chair, feels strange.

We get right down to it. I read to her from my journal.

"The day started out bad. I wrote, Olive Hudson, orphan. Olive Hudson, the new girl in town who has no friends. Olive Hudson, the girl who would give anything to get her old life back."

"Well," she says, and waits. Tess knows how to wait. I want her to say something, but I know she wants me to say something.

I look at the words:

> orphan
> New girl
> No friends
> Would give anything to get her old life back

"People are nice here," I say. I mention the puppies.

"Puppies!" Tess says.

"And when I was holding the little dog, Lumie, I didn't think about anything but her. I wasn't hurting; I wasn't lonely or scared."

"Olive, as you look at the list you made, how do you feel about those words?"

Awful. They are awful words.

"Would you change any of them? Add to them?"

I don't want to give a fast answer. I study the word

orphan. "I'd like to add to this—but I live with my sister, and my grandmother lives three hours away. I'm not alone in the world."

"Write that down," she says.

I do, and that feels better. I move to *New girl.* . . . Well, honestly, this happens to loads of girls, and being a new girl doesn't mean you won't find friends; it just means you need to find your way around a place and that takes time. I write *Chill* by that.

No friends—"Well, if we're defining friends as humans, I have met one boy who loves dogs like me. I have three new puppy friends and there are two great people who work with Maudie, Brian and Christine. Plus, I now, for the first time ever, live in a house with a rabbit."

Tess laughs. "Well done!" and I write down what she said. The hardest words for me to deal with might be *Would give anything to get her old life back.* A deep ache comes over me, an ache for my dad. Hearing his voice coming into the house, watching him stare at a mosquito and say, "Sorry, pal, nothing personal," before slapping it dead.

I'm quiet.

Tess finally says, "When we have to make a big

change, it's so tempting to want to leap right into it, but the best way to change your life is a few steps at a time. A few people at a time."

Then Tess says, "I'm proud of you. You're doing great, hard work."

I write that down in capital letters.

13

We Have a Situation Here

OVER THE NEXT two days, I help Jordan get Lumie, Leo, and Lightning ready for their raisers' homes.

"You guys are all hero dogs," I tell them, and they like that a lot.

I'm not going to un-love Lumie—I'm just going to live with missing her. It's like what we learned at camp about grieving. Grief is normal.

Grief isn't just sadness. You can be grieving and still have a good day. You can be happy about seeing a butterfly. You can pick up a smooth rock and make it dance across the water.

Lumie seems to be the perfect puppy for me, but this Northeast Guide Dog Center has big rules. I'm going to follow them.

I study the book on being a puppy raiser even harder than before.

I study a book on dog behavior.

Lumie keeps looking to me. I'm her go-to person. This high school person better be close to perfect. She'd better love you with everything she's got!

The night before Lumie gets picked up, Maudie sits me down.

"I've been thinking," she says.

This is good or bad, depending.

"Actually, it's been more than thinking: I've taken some action." She pauses. "I broke up with Roger."

"You're kidding." I'm trying not to do the happy dance.

"He needs me to be a different person than the one I am."

"You did the right thing."

"It's still hard. I'm going to have to get used to not being engaged. I know you didn't see the good things about him. . . ."

I put my hand on the table in case she wants to hold it. She takes my hand, only for a second.

That's when her phone pings. "It's Brian," she says. Maudie listens and bites her lip. "Wow, I'm not sure," she says. "I don't know if that could work. I have to think."

I'm getting worried.

Maudie says, "Would you like to talk with her?" She hands me the phone.

Why does Brian want to talk to me?

"Hi," I say.

"So listen, Olive. We have a situation here. I almost didn't call, because there are lots of things that would need to come together for it to work."

"What happened?"

"The girl who was going to raise Lumie had a death in the family. Her uncle. They have to go to Germany for the funeral and they'll be gone for two weeks."

I've stopped breathing for a minute.

"Olive?" Brian says. "Are you there?"

I breathe. "Yes."

"Here's the situation. People at the center feel another raiser should step in."

"For two weeks?" I ask.

"For the year. Since it's this high school girl's first time as a raiser, we feel she should wait for a puppy from another litter after she and her family are back from Germany."

Maudie is looking at me. I'm standing up now, straight as anything. I don't even dare to think—

"We need to make a very fast decision here. You and Maudie will have to talk this through."

"We're just now talking," I say. This is not exactly untrue.

"Well, if you would like to raise Lumie, this might be your moment."

I am bouncing now, bouncing because I feel like a million fireworks just went off.

"I would absolutely, totally, and completely like to. Yes."

"You need to talk this over seriously with Maudie. Lumie would need to come live with you in two days."

"What?" Maudie says.

Brian says he'll need to know soon.

"I can do soon! Soon is, like, one of my specialties."

Olive's Rules for How to Help an Adult
See Things from a Kid's Perspective

1. Smile.
2. Say, I know you remember what it was like to be my age—even if they don't, they probably won't admit it.
3. Keep smiling.
4. Say, I want this to work for everybody. Do not add, especially me.
5. Stand there smiling until they fold.

14

A+

I NUKE AN almond croissant for seven seconds and hand it to Maudie. She takes a bite—almond is her favorite.

"This is excellent. But you realize that any one of the residents here can say no to Lumie coming."

"I know."

I smile.

Maudie gets emotional. "I just don't want you to be hurt; you've had so many hard things happen."

"But if I don't try for the things I care about, I won't ever get them."

I wait—waiting is the hard part. You have to let the quiet do its work.

Maudie grabs a yellow pad and a blue pen.

"We're going to think this through."

She draws a dog, a cute one, at the top of the page.
She writes:

> *Reasons to do this . . .*

Below that she writes:

> *Reasons not to do this . . .*

Under "Reasons to do this" she writes:

> *Olive loves dogs*

I take the pen and add:

> **Olive is committed to dogs and knows that
> working with dogs will be her life's work.
> Plus, she wants to help someone.**

Maudie writes:

> *Olive is loyal and knows about commitment*
> *Olive has time this summer, but this*
> *commitment would go beyond that.*

I take the pen and add:

> We can work that out. Maybe the puppy could
> come to school.

> I doubt that.
> I think we're messing up our list.

Under "Reasons not to do this," Maudie writes:

> Heartbreak

She draws a sad heart with a break in it, leans back,
and looks at me.

Heartbreak is a big word, and the heart Maudie drew
really looks miserable. I'm not going to lie and say, Oh, no
big deal. I can handle it.

A list only works if you're honest.

I write:

> I want to raise a dog who can help someone
> who needs that dog more than me. I know
> that heartbreak is part of it, but I still
> want to do it.

I pour Maudie more coffee. She sniffs it like a dog.

This means she's thinking. I feel this is my moment. I write:

No one on Earth can raise Lumie like me.

I think she's folding, but to make sure . . .

This is living large.

I add:

You know this is true.

Maudie laughs. "Let's go talk to Lu Lu."

I BRING MY GDC folder, open it at the kitchen table, and say, "I'd like to walk you through a day in the life of a guide puppy in—"

I didn't expect Lu Lu Pierce to say, "You know, I saw Brian Ramsey earlier today and he asked me if we had any rules that would prohibit a guide dog puppy from living here."

I drink some OJ and begin to choke.

Maudie glares at me, but I can't stop choking. It's not a death choke, I don't think, but it sounds like one.

"Put your head down," Lu Lu says.

"No," Miss Nyla says, "hold it back."

I really don't want to choose sides here, but I do want to survive. Maudie gets behind me and whacks me on the back, which stops the choking, and I think I cough up something I had for dinner last week. She's that strong.

I take out one of the brochures with an adorable puppy on the front and say, "As you can see, the benefits of doing this would be—"

Then Mr. Burbank comes over with Bunster hopping by his side and Lu Lu tells him the situation. He looks at his rabbit, "How'd you feel about having some four-legged company?" Bunster hops off immediately. Mr. Burbank says, "If it were up to me, I'd say, let the puppy come, but Bunster is voting with his feet."

I think that means no.

I can't believe it!

We lose because of the rabbit vote?

I look to Lu Lu Pierce. "Lester," she tells him, "pets don't get to vote."

Miss Nyla says, "If Bunster were doing something

for humanity, he'd have a voice here." She takes out her phone. "I'm sending a message to Mark and Cora in 3B—they sleep late." She's typing, **do you like puppies?**

A ping. **yes!!!**

Mrs. Dool from 2C walks in slowly.

I turn the page in my GDC folder and say, "As you can see, a guide dog puppy is—"

Mrs. Dool sits down. Miss Nyla says, "Nothing much changes around here, Clara, and we're aiming to fix that."

"Good," Mrs. Dool says. "Do what you've gotta do." She gets up and heads out the door slowly.

"That's a yes." Miss Nyla smiles.

Lu Lu says, "We'd be delighted to house the puppy."

I close my presentation folder.

I'd say I get an A+ on that.

15

Focus

"OKAY, OLIVE, THE big goal here is to start training you," Brian says.

"I know about dogs."

I'm thinking of all the dogs I've walked and all the money I've made. I'm thinking about our old dog, Bitsy, and how I would take care of her when she was sick.

"I know you do," Brian says. "But there are specific training rules that you need to learn, and some might seem a little strange to you."

"What do I do then?"

"You ignore what you know and you do what the training manual tells you to do."

"Oh . . ."

"Because, at the end of the day, as much as you love Lumie and she loves you, she's not your dog. She's the center's dog. And we're trusting you to follow our rules so she can do her best. Okay?"

"Yes." This sounds pretty serious. I raise my hand.

Brian nods to me like a teacher. "Yes?"

"What if I mess up?"

"I really like that you asked that question, because not everyone does. That tells me a lot about how hard you'll try. But on messing up, we've all done it. We're not perfect."

"Except for me." It's Jordan walking in. He laughs.

"What we ask, Olive, is that if you make a mistake, you let us know. Just like Jordan has."

"There's a big space at the bottom of the monthly report so you can write up everything," Jordan tells me.

"So," says Brian, "Olive, right now, what do you see?"

Jordan waves.

"I see him," I say.

"Doing what?"

"Um. Waving. Being kind of difficult."

Jordan makes a stupid face.

"So if you were walking a puppy outside and you saw Jordan doing those things, what would you do?"

I shrug. "I don't know."

"Think about it."

"I guess . . . I'd ignore him and help the dog focus on me."

"Good," Brian says. "You could give the dog a treat and just walk by the distraction like it isn't there. Your body language means everything. Walk back and forth across the room."

I stand tall to be confident, and walk. I don't want to fail power walking. I trip because I'm nervous.

"Is that how you'd walk with a puppy?"

"I think so, except for the tripping."

"Walk with more purpose and make sure you see everything around you without losing focus."

I do that.

"Now, concentrate on your breathing, and I want you to say to yourself, 'I'm confident and I'm in control.'"

I guess I'm supposed to do this without feeling stupid or moving my lips.

"How did that feel?"

Lumie has stopped playing and is watching me. "It felt better. I felt stronger."

"And here is something I can't stress enough, Olive. The dog will sense how you're feeling. As much as you

can, learn to be confident and strong when you're walking." Brian smiles. "I used to walk like a bit of a bozo back
in the day."

"I can't believe that."

"The dogs have taught me a lot," he says. "I used to
work at a couple of big ad agencies, but they didn't let you
bring dogs. So I started my own agency."

goodWorks is the right name for this place!

I look at Lumie and she looks right back at me. She's
got the deepest eyes; it's like you can look in her eyes and
absolutely know she's a winner.

"One more thing. You and Maudie are on board for
puppy-proofing the house?"

"Hands and knees," I assure him.

I've done a lot of research on this.

To a puppy, *everything* is a chew toy.

Olive's Rules for Puppy-Proofing Your House:
Get these off the floor or out of jumping range:

shoes

paper

pencils

pens

food of any kind

medicine bottles

plants (NOTE: some can be poisonous!)

ribbon

anything in the trash

anything in your book bag, including your book bag

magazines

rugs (Okay: they need to stay on the floor)

towels

TP

tissues

napkins

pillows

all clothing, especially your favorite sweater (NOTE:
it's always your favorite sweater)

slippers

socks

your homework (NOTE: teachers are no longer accept-
ing, "My puppy ate my homework" as an excuse)

Cover all electrical cords, get outlet protectors.

Remember, puppy-proofing your home isn't a one-
time thing. It's a never-ending job. You have to
be consistent.

Remember, being consistent is exhausting.

16

Special Delivery

MAUDIE IS ON her hands and knees puppy-proofing our apartment. I'm following after her getting all that she missed.

Already, I'm seeing certain things that shout, Problem! I put sticky note warnings on those.

Our furry white chair that Maudie covered with fake fur gets a note. I write, Will Lumie rip this to shreds?

The pink-and-gold braided rug: Is this a major teething opportunity?

Maudie's emergency chocolate container behind the couch. Chocolate is poison for dogs. I write: No-brainer, just as Maudie grabs it from me and puts it on the top shelf of our bright green bookcase. She sets a stuffed koala on top of it.

"Safe," she says.

I smile innocently.

Maybe not.

This is chocolate, after all.

All I can think about is, Dad, I wish you could meet Lumie. You would love this little dog.

I have an entire schedule for her. A big goal in the beginning is to train her to be housebroken and poop in one outside place.

I have to help her get used to a new home and not miss her mom, brothers, and sisters.

Maudie looks under the furniture to make sure there isn't anything around that would hurt Lumie.

It just hits me how much my sister is doing for me.

"Maudie. You know what?"

"What?" Maudie looks up and clunks her head on a table.

"You're the best."

She rubs her head and picks a pen off the floor. She looks up at me—she's wearing her hair down these days, not pulled back tight, and something about her face seems prettier, softer. I crawl faster to catch up and hug her. She hugs me back. It's hard to hug this way; you lose your balance, as I'm doing right now. I fall over like a new puppy, and Maudie starts laughing.

She grins. "You ready?"

I've never been more ready for anything in my life!

A HORN HONKS OUTSIDE.

"She's here!"

I tear down the winding stairs and out the front door just as the puppy van pulls up.

Christine is driving and I'm so glad. "Special delivery!" She jumps out and heads to the back of the van.

Yes, so very special!

Every part of my heart is overbeating.

I wonder if you can have a heart attack from absolute happiness?

That would be so unfair, so I decide you can't. I stand here, hugely mature. I'm not going to look like some emotional case who can't handle my feelings.

From the back of the van, Christine takes Lumie out of her crate.

Maudie stands on the porch, grinning.

"Lumie," Christine says, "you are one exceptionally

lucky dog—you get to live with Olive and Maudie."

Well, all my needing to be mature goes out the window, let me tell you, because (and I don't think it's my imagination) when Lumie sees me, she kind of goes crazy, like seeing me is the best thing in her life. She leans toward me so I can hold her, and I say, "Ohhhhhhhhh!"

Maudie says the exact same thing.

I am hugging Lumie now, and I don't care who is watching, because we're going to do this right to help her feel at home from the very first second. I'm going to get an A+ in puppy raising.

Lumie licks my face and tries to chew my hair. I laugh. I tell Christine, "I'm going to be so careful! I won't mess up, I swear."

Christine lifts a crate and a bag with a picture of dog paws out of the van. "Among the things I'm worried about in this complicated world, you messing up, Olive, is not on the list."

Lu Lu Pierce and Mr. Burbank are waiting on the front porch. Mr. Burbank is holding Bunster, who does not look happy.

"That's a rabbit," I tell Lumie. "Your neighbor. He was here first. You're going to be good with other animals, I know it."

Mrs. Dool is watching us from the side of the house. Everyone at the Stay Awhile knows to not make a big deal about Lumie coming, because it will confuse her.

Brian told me, "This is a transition—not a party."

Me, I'd have balloons and a DJ to celebrate, but I get how every new thing needs to seem natural.

I put Lumie down and attach her leash to her collar. Eight-week-old puppies are really bad at walking on a leash. We stop about twenty-nine times before we reach the porch because there is a lot to explore.

Smells.

Grass.

Flowers.

Bushes.

Repeat.

Lumie almost pees on the flowers and bushes, but I say, "No," and take her over to her special poop-and-pee place that Miss Nyla made. It's under the flowering bush near the big tree.

We almost make it. Lumie pees on the bush, not under it.

Sorry! The problem with the poop-and-pee place is that I will have to duck under the bush so I can pick up the poop. But I'm not complaining. I'm not telling anyone that Lumie's name is misspelled, either. Miss Nyla made such a sweet sign: LUMEY'S PLACE.

I'm just feeling loved and grateful.

We're at the front steps. They're not steep and there are only three of them, so she can get up on her own, I think. Lumie sniffs the steps as Lu Lu Pierce puts her hand over her heart and says, "She's darling."

Christine gets in the van, honks, and drives off. Bunster is focused on Lumie and is struggling to be free.

Mr. Burbank looks at his rabbit: "This is another species. Work hard to get along." He puts Bunster down, but I have a carrot for him, and I hold it out. "This is from Lumie." Bunster thinks about this and takes it in his mouth. We've made peace. At least a little.

I'm telling Lumie everything we're walking past.

This is the door . . .

The hall . . .

The stairs . . .

We live upstairs, but we cook down here.

And this big room is the great room, which is not puppy-proofed!

"This is the staircase, which won't be easy to climb at

first." I point up. "We live on the second floor." Lumie is quiet for maybe three seconds then she wants to try the stairs. "I think I'd better carry you."

No. She wants to do it. "Do you want to walk upstairs?"

"That might be too much," Maudie says.

Lumie stands at the bottom stair and looks up. She shakes her head and tries to hop up on the first step. She falls back down. She tries this three times and gets up three steps. She starts whining.

"That was completely excellent," I tell her. "I'll give you a ride the rest of the way."

I don't know how to explain how good it feels to carry a puppy upstairs to my apartment. I'm not going to rush this—I carry her slowly and stand at our door. I point to the 2B—"That's us."

Lumie sniffs the 2B.

"That's good to do, learn the smell."

I unlock the door and we walk inside. Maudie follows with the crate and the dog bag. She sets the crate up by the couch, like we decided, and puts the gorilla chew toy I bought long ago inside.

Lumie looks around—so many new things. I let her sniff. She goes right up to the furry white chair. Uh-oh . . .

But all she does is look at it, like it might be a friend.

"That's a chair," I tell her. "Normally chairs aren't fuzzy. It's good you picked up on that. But the rules for guide dog puppies are that you can't be on the furniture, even if it's furry."

She lies down and makes a tiny whine.

I kneel next to her. "I know. This isn't home for you yet." I rub her tummy. "It's not home for me yet either, girl."

17

Middle of the Night

I EXPECTED THE crying—Brian said it would happen.

I didn't expect so much of it.

Poor Lumie. She misses her mom and her brothers and sisters.

I drag the blanket from my bed and go out to be with her. I hand her a toy, but she doesn't want it. I let her come out of the crate and be on my lap. I cover her just a little with the blanket and say, "I know. I know."

I say it because I do know.

I know what it's like to be in an all-new place with nothing familiar.

I know what it's like to miss the ones you love.

"But you love me, Lumie. We've been friends for eight days."

I take a picture of her and send it to Becca, who has not been having a good week.

Becca writes back: *ohhhhhhhhhhhhhhhhhhh!!!*

I tell Lumie, "You just made someone you don't know feel good."

Lumie sniffs my phone.

She cries and there's not much I can do except be here with her. "It gets better, you'll see. Change hurts like crazy, but you and me, we've got a big job to do. You're going to be a guide dog and change somebody's life. How amazing is that?"

I remember how Lumie would sleep close with Leo and Lightning—sometimes her head would be on one of their backs. I wonder if she needs me to lie down so she can cuddle close. I do that.

"You want to come closer here? I'm pretty warm. Not warm like another puppy, but warm for a human."

She doesn't exactly. But after a while of rubbing and talking quietly, she goes to sleep.

She wakes up crying, which I think means she has to go outside. I'm not supposed to do this at night without

Maudie. I try to wake Maudie, who is sleeping so hard, she could be in a fairy tale.

"Maudie, the dog has to go out."

Maudie makes a noise and turns over. This isn't good. Normally, I would open the blinds and let the sun in, but it's the middle of the night.

"Maudie," I say louder than normal, "we can have dog pee in the apartment or . . ."

Maudie opens one eye and makes a noise. I turn the light on. Lumie is crying. Maudie sits up. "Okay. Okay."

She puts on her shoes, carries Lumie outside, takes her to her poop spot, and bends down, which is going low for Maudie.

"Did she do it?" I ask.

"I can't tell."

"You feel around with the bag." I shine a flashlight so she can see.

Maudie says, "I used to be an interesting person."

"I think you're interesting. Not at this exact moment, but in general."

Lumie pees on Maudie's hand and trots over to me.

"We're going to work on aim," I tell her. "But that was pretty good for three in the morning."

Maudie and I try to get back to sleep, but Lumie is

sniffling, so Maudie brings her blanket to our living room and lies down on the couch, which is not long enough for her to lie on. She joins me on the floor.

"I think she misses her mom," I say.

Maudie puts her hand over Lumie's little back. The lights are out, but I can see in the dark, though not as well as a dog.

All I know about my mom is what people have told me. Grandma said that my mom wanted to travel the world. She gave Dad a globe that he kept on his dresser next to Maudie's picture.

Maudie and I have that globe on a table by our couch. Dad said Mom never traveled far, but she was an adventurer. She had her passport ready, even though she didn't ever get to use it.

"You never talk about your mother, Maudie."

She's quiet and Lumie gets quiet too. This puppy has managed to get two females to lie on the floor with her. That's a big accomplishment for the first night in a new place.

I want to know about this sister, this half sister of mine. Maybe after all she's given up for me, I shouldn't think of her as half a sister anymore. . . .

"Do you see your mom?" I ask.

Maudie takes a quick breath. "Not too much. My mother isn't an easy person."

"Oh."

I don't want to ask the wrong question, because some things are so private, you have to wait to be invited in.

"She has a lot of problems," Maudie adds.

"I'm sorry."

"After the divorce, it was just me and Mom. She was depressed. She didn't want me to see Dad. She hated him." Maudie says so quietly, "I did too, for a long time."

How could anyone hate Dad? I'm not sure we should keep talking about this.

"I didn't see him much until I was older. I met you, too, when I was sixteen. You were a baby."

"I don't remember my time as a baby."

"There's a picture somewhere of me holding you."

I bite my lip. "What was I doing?"

"Crying."

"Sorry."

Lumie starts to cry a little. Maudie tells her, "It's okay. It's going to be okay."

I have to ask. "Did you meet my mom?"

"Yes, I did."

"Did you like her?"

"Well, not exactly. She was nice and she was funny, I remember that. But I wanted Dad to be married to my mom, so I resented her."

The clock reads 4:11 a.m.

"This is some slumber party, Olive. We should go to sleep."

I try to sleep, but I can't.

I keep thinking of the song we wrote the last night in our old house.

> *I believe in you*
> *I really do*
> *And because that's true*
> *I'm betting on you*

I listen for Maudie's sleeping sounds. . . .

"Maudie?"

"What?"

"Are you awake?"

"Kind of . . ."

"What did your mom tell you about Dad?"

I hear her turn over. "I don't think we should—"

"I want to know."

She sighs. "She said he was selfish."

I sit up. "He's the least selfish person ever!"

"You asked me what she said. She had lots of problems and she blamed him for everything wrong in the universe. She said we couldn't trust him."

Your mother sounds awful, Maudie. Completely and terribly awful!

"It's what I heard growing up," she explains. "Dad wasn't around to counter it."

"Where was he?"

"I don't know exactly."

Here we are on the floor with all the lights out; the window frames the dark sky. It's easier to talk into the night and not have to see a person's face sometimes— you just say your words and let them say theirs.

I finally hear Maudie's sleeping sounds.

I couldn't possibly sleep.

My thoughts come out like lines of a poem. I learned at camp that when that happens, pay attention.

Hold it close.

Write it down.

It's trying to teach you something.

Do you love me, Maudie?

I'm not sure you do.

If you asked me if I loved you, I'd say, Yes.

I started out feeling grateful

for all you've done for me.

I loved my dad with everything I had.

After he died, I needed to fill myself back up again.

I love how you step up.

I love how you're brave.

I love how you are making us a home in this

crazy house.

I love how you draw funny animals on the

LIVE LARGE sign and make me laugh.

I love how you said yes to raising Lumie.

Lots of people would have said no.

I love how you are on the floor right now

when you could be sleeping in your bed.

I wonder, maybe, if love isn't just something you're born

feeling toward another person;

Maybe it's also something you decide on.

Not like deciding if you want chocolate or strawberry ice

cream . . .

More like, I want to love you.

In the beginning of our beginning,

I had to work at it.

Push it and shove it into place a little until

    it obeyed.

But now, for me, it's a natural thing.

It's there when I wake up and when I go to sleep.

I hope you feel that too.

18

Good Girl

CAN I EVER really feel that Lumie is not my dog?

She is squatting in her pooping place and I'm saying, "Good girl." I brush a low branch away and pick up after her. "You're really doing well at this," I tell her. "I'm impressed." Lumie wags her tail and I tell her, "I'm here to help you get ready to do big things in the world."

Lumie sniffs the ground.

"I'm learning a lot about what blind people need—things I never once thought of, like the reason you have to always poop in one place is so when you get your blind companion, you'll be trained to do this and they can clean up after you. They don't ever want to leave a mess behind. Come over here."

A squirrel runs by and Lumie is ready to chase it. Distraction is one of the worst things for a guide dog puppy.

"No squirrels," I tell her. "You have to focus. Look here."

Another squirrel scurries up a tree and Lumie pulls at her leash. "No," I say, "look at me." I put my face right in front of hers. "See how cute I am? Good girl."

Maudie pulls up in the van. She's wearing a purple-and-yellow scarf she made from a piece of fabric. She can make anything.

It's Saturday morning. We're going to take Lumie for a ride and get her used to a plumbing van that probably still smells like our dad.

Getting Lumie used to new things is how she learns to be brave in the world. My dad said that every time we learn something, we grow a little. I mentioned this to Maudie.

"Maybe this explains my height."

Nothing I've seen can explain her height, since Dad wasn't tall, and I'm not, and she told me that her mother wasn't tall. We get in the van, and I don't know why it feels like memories are hanging from the rearview mirror and sitting in the back seat, whispering.

Today, I make the list in my head for what I've got.

Love—check

Excitement—check

Hope—check

A stomachache from eating too many
      Cheez-Its—check

A loneliness about my mom—check

A deep missing of Dad—double check

Gratitude for Maudie—double check

Lumie is looking out the window as Maudie drives.

Maudie says, "I got a phone call yesterday."

The way she says it doesn't sound good.

"It's complicated," she adds.

"A lot of our life is complicated," I say.

"If you don't want to do this—fine."

"I won't know, Maudie, unless you tell me."

"Your aunt Ceil and your cousin, Gina, are going to be in the area. . . ."

My stomachache gets worse.

Maudie coughs. . . . "And they would like to come by and say hello."

"No."

"I understand why you would say that."

"No. They can't see Lumie."

"The problem is, Olive, she didn't ask—she told me. They are stopping by today at four."

"We don't have to be there." I hold Lumie tighter. "No negative people."

"You want me to call her back?"

"Yes. Say we're heading to Alaska."

"She might not believe that."

"Okay—I'm thinking of a map of America. Say we're in New Hampshire."

"What if she wants to reschedule?"

"We can't. We're moving to England."

"Olive. This is not going to solve the problem. What if they're trying to make things right?"

I can see Gina's face at the funeral and hear her awful words that I never told anybody:

What's it feel like to be an orphan?

Here's the one thing my dad was 100 percent wrong about: He said Gina was my only cousin and I had to be nice to her. No matter what.

But doing that just made her hate me more.

Being quiet about it now isn't helping, so I tell Maudie what Gina said to me at the funeral.

She stops the van. Looks at me. "How dare she!" I hold Lumie close as some of that hurt comes back, but not all. "I don't want you being a victim," she said. "We are not seeing visitors today."

Works for me.

We drive around town in the van so Lumie can see it. We walk down by the red bridge crossing and look at the swans. Mostly, Lumie likes the squirrels. I love this red bridge. Maudie takes a picture of it.

Then we drive across Caitlin's Bridge, which can only take one car at a time.

Maudie calls Aunt Ceil, who says the next time they're in town, they'll give us more notice.

Whew.

We head home at two o'clock.

At two thirty, when I am sitting on the front porch with Mr. Burbank and Bunster, Aunt Ceil and Gina pull up in their car, smiling and waving.

"We just thought we'd take a chance and swing by a little earlier and here you are," Aunt Ceil says.

I'm trying to remember everything Tess said to do when I was with them.

"It's hard to understand," Tess told me, "but some people, no matter what you do, want to be superior and

put you down. As tough as it is, try not to take it personally, because they will do this with lots of people. It's not
about you."

This is great advice when Aunt Ceil and Gina are not
getting out of their car and walking up the stairs to see
me. I know that mean expression on Gina's face too—
the one she always gets when she's going to say something awful.

I stand up and look at Bunster.

Why can't you be a fierce guard rabbit and protect
me?

Aunt Ceil looks at the Stay Awhile and says, "Well,
isn't this . . . charming?"

She doesn't mean charming. She means, Wow, you
guys used to have your own house and now you're living
here.

Gina says, "Do you have to sleep in a tent?"

I never know what to say back to her. I always think
of something the next day.

"I suppose your father didn't really leave enough for
you to live on," Aunt Ceil says.

You know what? That's enough!

Lu Lu Pierce sweeps in wearing a gold-and-red dhuku.

She looks like a great queen you'd better not mess with and she says, "Well, I see you have guests, Olive. Would you ladies like a tour of the house?"

"No," Gina says.

"Of course we would," Aunt Ceil says.

And Lu Lu Pierce tells her, "We have one rule here in our community. Kindness. Do you have any questions so far?"

I almost laugh out loud. That was good!

Gina looks down and Aunt Ceil's smile is so fake, I think it's going to break her face.

Lu Lu Pierce waves her mighty hand. "All right then, ladies, please come this way! And do be careful. This is a historic and extremely important house."

Maudie comes out of the kitchen holding Lumie. "I'm sorry, Olive."

"Lu Lu's got your back," Mr. Burbank says.

Everything in me wants to hide Lumie, but I'm feeling stronger, like I want her to see this. I want Aunt Ceil and Gina to see the best guide dog puppy in America.

I hear Lu Lu say, "This is the great room, of course, and we have quite a library here—this is a gathering point for our community."

Twenty minutes later they come back to the porch. Gina sees Lumie and makes the "Ohhhhhhhhhhhh!" noise.

"Let me hold her!"

"No," I say. "She's too young."

"Come on, Olive!"

"No. Sorry. She's a special dog. She's in training."

"Yeah. Right. For what?"

"She's going to be a guide dog."

Gina starts laughing. "So you need a guide dog?"

"I'm raising her. It's a special job."

"And we're very proud of Olive," Maudie says. She has a way of using her full height and when she does, like now, it's wonderful.

"Lumie has to take a nap now," I say. "Thanks for stopping by."

"I'm glad you're not living with us," Gina says.

I smile. "I am too."

I turn and walk through the door.

I can feel her hate following me, but I know this:

Your hate can't stay here.

I won't let it.

See ya, Gina.

I nuzzle Lumie and head up the stairs. She wants to try to climb a few steps. I put her down. "Go for it," I say. Lumie pulls herself up three steps and looks back at me. "Good girl, Lumie." I give her a treat.

I walk to apartment 2B and add, "Good girl, Olive."

I give myself a chocolate.

19

A Job to Do

MAUDIE IS DOWNSTAIRS hanging one of her paintings in the great room. It's a different painting of sunflowers than she did for Dad's hospital room. I love that my mom grew sunflowers and Maudie seems to be connected to them too.

I'm betting Lu Lu Pierce was one of the world's best librarians. She has a corner library in this room and chairs all around for reading.

I want to make a list of all the people who have my back, which is one of those phrases people say but don't always think about. To me it means a person is there to help you. It's like they're watching for anything that could hurt you and you can count on them to step in when they see you're in trouble.

Here's my list:

Maudie

Brian

Christine

Lu Lu Pierce

Becca

Tess

Grandma

That's a lot of great people guarding one middle-school back.

I get Maudie's pillow from the bookshelf and lean against it. We never put it on the floor because Lumie would shred it to pieces.

I sit up straight and look at Lumie, asleep in her crate. She's so small—it's hard to imagine that in a year she could be a mighty guide dog. Puppies are the cutest, but they have to learn and grow and I get to be part of that.

I smile. A guide dog has their owner's back.

"You're going to learn how to do that, girl."

There's so much hate in the world, but that's why a kid has to make lists. To remind you who you've got, what you've got, and who you are.

Lumie wakes up, sniffs the air, and starts to whine.

Poop time.

I'm pretty sure Aunt Ceil and Gina have left, but if they haven't, I don't care. I've got a job to do.

"Come on, girl."

She trots out of her crate.

"In case you're wondering, I've got your back." I rub her back to get the idea across.

Lumie bounds for the door and we head down the stairs. Mr. Burbank is still on the porch. I'm a little embarrassed that he had to see all that happened with my aunt and cousin.

"That girl must be so jealous of you," he says.

"Oh." I look down. "I don't think so. She just hates me."

"Believe me, kid. She hates herself more."

I smile at him, but Lumie has to pee.

When I go back upstairs, I'm going to add Mr. Burbank to the list.

I'm having a seriously good day.

• • •

I SEE JORDAN at Brian's and he's just quiet.

I say hi and he doesn't say anything.

I say, so what's been going on?

He shrugs.

I say, any new puppies?

I say, how's your leadership program?

I even say, you look more like a leader than you did last week. The program must be working, figuring he'll laugh. He doesn't.

Then I say the right thing. "What's wrong?"

I sit next to him in the goodWorks cafeteria and he doesn't get up and walk away. He sighs.

"My new doctor agrees with the old one."

"What's that mean?"

"Oh," he says, "I didn't tell you. I thought you knew."

He says it means his eyes are getting worse.

"I'm seeing a few more shadows. Just a few. But that will probably keep happening. Both my uncles have this."

"Wow, Jordan, I'm sorry."

He looks straight ahead.

I think about all the wrong things people have said to me.

"Well, you be courageous now. Your dad needs that from you."

Actually, Dad needed me to be honest.

"You're an orphan now."

I am what I decide I am.

I tell this to Jordan, who shakes his head. "Someone actually called you an orphan?"

"At the funeral."

"That's bad. Okay, so if the doctors are right, and doctors can be wrong, and if my eyes get worse, a lot worse, please do not ever say to me, 'How many fingers am I holding up?'"

"I promise I will never ask you that."

"Also, never say you feel sorry for me or that I'm inspiring."

"I'll try, but you are inspiring sometimes, so you might have to get over that one."

Jordan smiles. "What should I never say to you?"

I sigh. "Oh, well, the big one is, I know how you feel."

"I will never say that."

"And don't ask me how I'm doing."

Jordan nods.

"And one more: don't say, 'Please let me know if there's anything I can do for you.'"

"Really? That sounds like a good one."

"But I'm not going to let you know if there's anything

you can do. Right? You need to think of something you can do."

Jordan is thinking. . . .

"You know, like, bringing me a year's supply of choco-late or giving me a lot of money."

He laughs. "You're okay, Olive."

"You're okay too."

Lumie comes over and nuzzles Jordan's hand. "What dog is this?" he asks.

He can't tell?

His eyes are that bad?

"It's Lumie, Jordan, and—"

He's laughing. "Kidding!"

"Don't do that!"

He breaks up laughing.

I want to tell him, whatever happens to your eyes, Jordan, I know you'll figure out what to do and have a seriously good life.

Maybe that's the wrong thing to say.

Would I want someone to say that to me?

Yes, I would, actually.

So I tell him.

And when I do, he stands up like energy just shot through him and he says, "You know what? Working with

GDC all these years has ruined me for ever giving up."

"That's pretty inspiring," I say. "Sorry."

He laughs. "Maybe I'll use that in my presentation. I have to give a speech about raising guide dog puppies and why I do it." He slumps. "There will be one hundred people in the room."

"That's a lot, but I bet you'll be awesome."

"I don't have to give it for a month."

"You've got lots of time to work on it."

"Or leave town," he says.

20

Fluff Happens

Socialization
Discipline
Rules
Face licking
Lots of hugs
Housebreaking
Reports

I'm probably overdoing it on my puppy raiser's reporting, but when I care about something, I just can't stop.

This week Lumie stopped crying at night for her dog family. I am happy to report that she sees us as her family now.

We made a mistake and left a big box of Kleenex on the floor and it was amazing how she shredded it and put it in small piles around the living room. She seemed proud when we found her doing it. I said no, because I caught her in the act, but she looked at me with her big eyes and I started laughing. Maudie took a lot longer to laugh.

Lumie has met a fireman, a baby, three butterflies, and a policeman giving out parking tickets. He took one look at Lumie, who cocked her head, and the policeman ripped up the ticket he was going to give to Maudie.

Lumie has spent several hours on the porch looking at Bunster, a lop-eared rabbit. who seems more nervous since she arrived.

Lumie likes the smell of coffee and my toes.

Lumie enjoyed tearing apart Maudie's "Happiness" presentation for Smiley Bank—but only the middle part that talked about looking for small moments of joy in each day.

Maudie then discovered that Lumie had dragged most of her Smiley Bank presentation, BELIEVE IN THE POWER OF A NEW DAY, under Maudie's bed and chewed it, according to Maudie, "into oblivion."

Maudie said, "I need this day to be over."

It was only nine a.m.

Thank you, Olive Hudson, puppy raiser.

Then for some reason, I start crying. I really miss Dad.

Lumie walks over and leans against my leg. She always comforts me when I cry, which I've been doing a lot lately. She steps right up to me and puts her head close to me. I don't know why I've been crying like this. I think I really miss Dad.

DAD HAD ONE of those signs that so many people do that reads: STUFF HAPPENS.

I'm not an artist like Maudie, but I make a sign on my computer that reads,

FLUFF HAPPENS

I put it above the door of Lumie's crate.

Maudie laughs when she sees it. "We might be able to sell that, Olive."

We are living large!

Maudie draws a FLUFF HAPPENS balloon on the LIVE LARGE poster.

But then the flowers come.

Yellow, pink, and white roses with a big bow. Gorgeous.

Then the card—one of those giant-sized cards—almost as big as Lumie. The front of it reads:

> You are in my thoughts every moment.
> When I wake and when I sleep.

Lumie sniffs the card, unimpressed.

Then Roger shows up.

He is back from Singapore. He pulls up to the Stay Awhile in his red car and jumps out. I'm on the porch rereading the GDC rule book.

"Hey, Olive. Long time no see."

Oh, this is really bad . . .

I close the book and put it in my backpack.

"So how are you?" He's smiling at me like he's glad to see me, which I know isn't true.

"I'm good." *And* bad.

"That's the dog?"

Obviously, Lumie is a dog, but I'm polite and say, "Yes, that's Lumie."

Roger, who is not any kind of animal person, crouches down and says, "Hey, Lumie."

Lumie sniffs his hand, backs away, and looks at me like, Who is this guy?

"Is your sister around? I've been trying to call her."

Just then Maudie stands in the door. She's wearing her long white artist shirt, jeans, sandals, and earrings that almost touch her shoulders. "I'm around," she says.

I don't like the way she says, "I'm around," either. She says it like she's been waiting around for him, which is so not true! I also don't like how beautiful she looks—like she was really working at it—which is not helping the situation.

Roger says, "I'm glad you're around."

I really want to leave this porch, but I think I should stay to protect Maudie, who is close to glowing.

Roger moves closer to Maudie and she moves closer to him, and I clap my hands really loud and say, "Yes, we're all around! How about that?"

Roger and Maudie look at me; Lumie sits, confused.

I hear Roger say, "I've missed you." I know he's not talking to me.

I hear Maudie say, "Really?"

And I'd like to shout, Maybe not. Maybe this is some kind of game he's playing.

Now I see Jordan walking up the driveway. I'm so glad to not be the only middle schooler here. "Thank you for coming!" I shout.

Jordan looks surprised. "Uh . . . sure . . ."

"Jordan, this is my sister's ex-fiancé, Roger."

A quiet kind of thud happens when I say that, but I'm glad I said it, because someone needed to.

Roger laughs nervously. "I hope we can get rid of the ex in front of fiancé."

Jordan sits down. "My sister has an ex-fiancé, but he never comes around."

Mr. Burbank walks out on the porch, sits in the rocking chair, and says, "Looks like it might rain."

Maudie says, "Roger, I'm not sure this is a great time to . . ."

That's when Roger, I'm not kidding, gets down on one knee and takes her hand as it starts to rain. He takes out a ring from his pocket, but accidentally drops it through a hole in the wooden porch and says a word, actually three words, I'm never supposed to say.

Mr. Burbank rocks. "I was right about the rain."

"Roger." That's Maudie.

Roger is trying to kick a bigger hole in the porch so he can get the ring back.

Jordan says, "My sister kept the ring."

Lumie is getting acclimated to romantic stress and probably developing new socialization skills. I'm not sure how to write this up on my raiser's report. Maybe:

> Lumie learns not to trust certain people even
> when they bring diamonds.

I want to shout at Maudie that she's not really a diamond person.

Maudie takes Roger's hand and says, "Come on, let's talk."

"I'll watch the ring," Mr. Burbank says. "I can see it shining down there."

Maudie and Roger go into the great room.

"Oops," Mr. Burbank says, "a squirrel's taking some interest. Get out of there." Mr. Burbank stomps his foot and the squirrel runs off. Lumie pulls at her leash to chase it.

"No squirrels, kid." Mr. Burbank sticks out his hand for Lumie to sniff.

I could use some big life advice right now, because Roger seems like he's desperate to get Maudie to marry him.

That's when we hear Maudie's voice get louder, and Roger's voice gets louder, and Jordan says, "You know what, Olive? I think it's going to be fine."

I get Dad's tool kit, remove one of the planks of wood on the porch, and rescue the engagement ring. Roger storms onto the porch muttering more bad words. I hand him the ring, and he drives away too fast in his red car.

Jordan says, "I think that went pretty well."

Maudie comes out on the porch, not glowing anymore.

Mr. Burbank looks at her, shakes his head, and says, "That guy? Nah . . ."

"I know," she says.

"Nice car, though," he adds.

Lumie goes over to Maudie and nuzzles her hand. Maudie rubs Lumie's back for the longest time.

I nail the wood plank back in place.

I like fixing things.

21

Leave It!

I AM PRACTICING confident walking like Brian taught me. I practice feeling I've got power inside and courage coming out of me. I march into our apartment and Maudie is playing her guitar, playing a slow, sad song that makes you want to have bad posture. But I stand tall.

"Hi," I say.

"Hi."

On the couch is artwork for Smiley Bank—the poster has all these squares and each square has a different person's smile—old people, young, babies.

Smile—your banker will know you by name.

Smile—we'll count your loose change.

Smile—we've got treats for your dog.

There's a picture of Lumie on the poster.

"I love this!" I shout.

Maudie looks down at her guitar.

I sit next to her. "If you want to talk about what happened with Roger, you can talk to me. Dad used to talk to me after he had a bad date, and lots of kids used to talk to me about things that were hard. I even had parents talk to me at the bus stop. I guess I'm just that kind of a person. I'm a really good listener, except when I interrupt."

Maudie strums her guitar. "I'm not sure I have all that much to say. I have to get used to my life without Roger."

I don't know what it's like to be almost engaged or why she would be sad that Roger is gone. I'd like to tell her something that can help.

"I know about giving up things I love, Maudie. I know how much it hurts."

I get my guitar, tune to hers. "We need a happy song." And together we sing one of Dad's favorites—a "gloom buster," he called it.

How are you doing today
There's something about this day
The sun's in the sky
And the air smells sweet
It's a good day
A good day
Hey—Hey

Lumie likes guitars and singing. She paws my tapping foot, which tickles. I start laughing and Lumie licks my toes. She goes over to Maudie's toes now, because Lumie doesn't want to leave anyone out. Maudie is seriously ticklish and she is laughing and strumming and Lumie leaps around.

How are you doing today
There's something about this day
The sun's in the sky
And the air smells sweet
It's a good day
A good day
Hey—Hey

Big strum to finish . . . *Hey!*

• • •

LUMIE IS READY to take her first walk into town. Before we head out, I stop in the kitchen to fill our water bottles. Mr. Burbank takes a rotisserie chicken out of a bag and puts it on a plate on the table. That's when Lumie stands on her little hind legs, leaps up, grabs the chicken, the plate crashes to the floor, and she drags the bird off.

"No!" I scream. "Lumie, leave it!"

She's more interested in eating the chicken than sitting.

It takes three "leave its" before she lets go.

Mr. Burbank takes his former lunch and throws it in the trash. "This is why I have a rabbit," he says. "Vegetarians don't do that."

"I'm sorry." I clean up the broken plate.

Lumie isn't looking like she learned much except that she loves the taste of rotisserie chicken. Mr. Burbank opens a can of tuna fish and waves us out the door.

"I'm sorry," I say again.

I tell Maudie what happened and she says we should get him another rotisserie chicken in town. Maudie is going with us on the first walk, even though she is a bridesmaid at her friend's wedding tonight, even though I can do this myself and town is only four blocks away!

I look at Lumie in her green guide-dog-in-training vest. "You look great, girl. All the things you've been learning? We're going to build on those. That's how you learn more." I stand with absolute confidence. Lumie looks at me. "Okay. We're doing this."

It takes forever to get there because Lumie stops at everything she sees.

I tell her . . .

That's an ant.

That's another ant. Fascinating, I know.

That's an anthill.

"That's a disgusting half-eaten hot dog someone threw on this road," Maudie mentions.

The ultimate distraction runs up a tree.

"Lumie, that's a squirrel," I tell her, "which you ignore exactly like a chicken."

Jordan is meeting us at Smiley Bank, which is one of the guide puppy–friendly places in town and a good-Works client. I like Jordan, but I'm feeling I can walk Lumie myself.

I'm heading down Main Street and see the big smiley face on Smiley Bank's roof. Honestly, I don't think smiley faces are what I want to see in a bank. I want to know the people who are guarding my money have their game faces on.

"Okay, we're crossing the street," I tell Lumie, who looks back at the curb, where it was safe. "Streets are for crossing. You can do this."

Lumie pulls away from me, which isn't good. I stop right there and say, "Lumie, heel."

She looks to see if I mean it. I say it again, and she trots across the street with me.

"Good dog!" Maudie says.

About sixteen people stop and smile and make the "Ohhhhhhhhhhhh!" noise.

I'm feeling pretty spectacular, I'm telling you, like I'm doing something important with my life. Jordan is waiting for us in front of the bank and Lumie gives him an extra tail wag.

"Good girl," he says. "You're looking strong."

Okay, we're going into the bank now, and Christine, Jordan, and Brian all told me, people are going to want information.

"Ohhhhhhhhhh!"

"How old is the puppy?"

—Twelve weeks, I tell them.

"You're with the guide dog group?"

—Yes, ma'am, this is my first time as a raiser.

"Well, good for you."

—Yes, ma'am.

"Can I pet her?"

—Um, I wish you could, but when she's wearing this vest, it means she's learning how to work, and so I'm sorry, you can't.

"Will she bite?"

I look to Jordan because I'm close to 100 percent sure the answer is no. She won't bite, but I don't want to do anything wrong.

"She won't bite," Jordan says.

We walk to the teller, who leans down smiling, and Lumie looks up at him. "Are you here to open an account?" the teller asks Lumie, who looks at me. I deposit my monthly check from Social Security that I've been getting since Dad died.

"You can come in anytime," the teller says.

I'm not sure I've ever seen so many people smiling in a bank. A little girl shouts, "Look, Mommy! It's a hero dog!"

Lumie wags her tail as the little girl says shyly to me, "I want to do what you're doing."

Jordan gives her a Guide Dog Center brochure and says, "You can when you're a little older."

"Yes!" the girl shouts.

Her mother says, "We'll see."

I'm thinking, Let her do it, ma'am, because she will never forget this. I kneel down to feel Lumie's back. She moves alongside me and leans into my leg, which is how she hugs.

"That's important when they do that," Jordan tells me, like I don't know this. I know what love feels like. "You're doing great," he says.

I know that too. I don't know why I can't do this by myself.

We walk out of Smiley Bank leaving sixteen smiling people. I bet even the faces of the presidents on the money are smiling.

I wonder why puppies aren't being sent to places where people are angry and don't know how to talk to each other.

Dad, here I am, having a major dog moment in a happy bank.

Can you and Mom see me from heaven?

22

It's Complicated

MAUDIE LOOKS MISERABLE, and there isn't time to sing the "Good Day" song.

The bridesmaid dress she is wearing was picked out by a person who wasn't thinking straight. Her friend Myra, the bride, is normally a reasonable person. You just don't know what stress can do to a bride, I guess.

The dress has long puffy sleeves and Maudie has to wear a floppy hat that has flowers on it.

"Just kill me now," she says as Lumie and I walk her to the car. Lumie likes the flowing part of the long dress—she keeps trying to catch it.

"Tell me the truth, Olive. Do I look stupid?"

I'm trying to think of a word other than stupid.

Dumb.

Brain-dead.

Those are worse.

I take a big breath. "You look pretty stupid, but you won't be the only one." There are three other bridesmaids.

Lumie takes a swipe at the hem of the dress as Maudie gets in the car.

"It will be over soon," I say, hoping that helps.

Actually, it was just beginning.

MAUDIE IS QUIET for a few days after that wedding. I don't think it's shock from wearing the world's worst dress, either.

She stands by the window looking out.

She sighs.

She draws flowers and a big cake on the LIVE LARGE.

Artists don't always communicate like other people.

I am working on being consistent with Lumie.

"No. You can't eat my shoe."

"No. You can't eat my sandwich."

"No. You can't chase Bunster. You really can't do that."

Then, five days after being a bridesmaid, Maudie says, "Roger was at the wedding."

Lumie and I turn to look at her.

She clears her throat. "We're talking."

What does that mean?

"It's complicated."

I already know that!

I have to say it. "He's not the right guy for you."

Her eyes flash. "You and Roger have not had a chance to get to know each other."

Should I tell her what Roger said to me at Dad's funeral?

Did being a bridesmaid, even in a bad dress, make her want to be a bride?

"This is my life, Olive. Things can work out when it seems like they can't."

Lumie looks at me, like, Say something.

"Why do you like him, Maudie?"

She looks at her hands. They're not manicured— she has strong hands. "In some ways, and this probably sounds strange, he completes me."

It does sound strange.

"Roger and I are opposites, but together we make a whole."

A whole what? I'm thinking back to geometry—isn't this like trying to attach a triangle to a circle? No way is that going to fit.

"Oh," I say.

Lumie whines. She needs to pee.

I take her outside to her place.

"Good girl."

Lumie looks at me.

"Are you picking up some weirdness upstairs? It's going to be okay."

I stand like I mean it, but I don't know if I do.

23

Here's the Truth

WHAT I'VE GOT today . . .

Love—double check
Power—check
Consistency—well . . .
Hope—I'm working at it.
Grief—check. I miss Dad.
Maturity—double check. I'm raising the
   best guide dog puppy in America.
Intense worry about my future involving
   Roger—quadruple check and three
   exclamation marks!!!

Maudie is singing around the house like a Disney princess whose dreams are about to come true.

She goes in the hall and says to Bunster, "Well, hello, neighbor. How are you this beautiful day?"

Bunster can't take this and thumps down the stairs.

I'm scared to do this, but I have to.

"Maudie, I need to tell you something."

She puts a pink scarf over her shoulders and half twirls by the window.

Wisely, I'm holding my journal and a strong cup of coffee. I hand the coffee to her.

She smiles and sips. "Mmmmmm . . ."

I take a big breath. "I haven't told anyone about this."

"Okay." She waits.

I begin. "Gina wasn't the only one who hurt me at the funeral. . . ." I open my journal to the day of the funeral and to what Roger said. "I wrote this down right after it happened. I dated it and even put in the time."

> 1:47 p.m. It was right after lunch. Roger said to me, "So, who are you going to live with?"
> Things hadn't been decided yet and I told him that.
> He said, "Just make sure it's a person who really wants you—otherwise . . ."

He let the "otherwise" hang there. Then he said,
"otherwise you'll have a very unhappy life."
He walked away and I felt like I'd been kicked
in the stomach.

Right below that was what I wrote about Gina asking what it felt like to be an orphan.

Maudie's whole face has changed. She puts her coffee down. She sits in the furry chair with my journal and reads the page again and again.

I gulp. "I swear this happened, Maudie. I—"

She holds up her hand like a policewoman stopping traffic. "I believe you." She closes the journal. I look up at our ceiling that Maudie painted sky blue with a few puffy clouds.

This is not a puffy cloud moment.

"Olive. If I could go back and erase these cruel words that were said to you, I would."

I nod.

"I had no idea he would ever say something like this. And I promise you, I have no interest in committing to a man who would say something like this. But I have to know—why didn't you tell me?"

I'm not completely sure. "I didn't think I had the right."

"You always have the right to tell me anything, especially when someone hurts you."

This seems like a really good time for sisters to hug. And we do.

Over the next days, Roger calls, and tries to explain. On Friday he shows up in his red car.

Maudie meets him on the porch. "You made a long drive for nothing."

Lu Lu Pierce and Mr. Burbank are on the porch, too. I'm in our bedroom, right above the porch, with the windows open. I can hear really well.

Roger says, "Can we talk privately?"

One floor up, I shake my head.

"No," Maudie says.

Roger says, "Look, we need to get married. Isn't there somewhere else the kid can live?"

If I had a water balloon, I'd drop it on his head.

Maudie says, "No." She's getting really good at saying that.

Roger pushes. "You want that limitation in your life?"

"I want Olive in my life," she tells him. "Not you."

Lumie wags her tail.

Bye-bye, Roger.

24

Helping

I'M NOT SURE how the middle of August happened.

Lumie is now fourteen weeks old and she is one of eleven guide dog puppies in training who are running and playing in Brian's backyard. This is our puppy club. The little ones, like Lumie, stay together and jump and play. The older ones calm the younger ones, as the puppy raisers talk to each other while watching our dogs at the same time.

"I'm wondering," I say to Christine, "if you can give me some advice about . . ."

"Misty, down. No!" Christine shouts.

"Um . . . I'm just worried that I might not be doing everything right, and—"

"Lightning—no! Good dog."

Back to me. "I was just wondering what it was like for you with your first puppy."

"Okay, kids—time-out!" That's Brian, who is separating two dogs.

This is great training to keep focused no matter what—training for a person, I mean!

Brian comes over: now I have two adults to talk to. I tell them about Lumie stealing Mr. Burbank's rotisserie chicken. Then I ask, "How do I train her not to counter surf?"

"Ah," Brian says, "the temptation of meat."

"She keeps pulling toward the counter and the table when we're in the kitchen."

Brian knows almost everything. "I'd suggest you go bold. Put hamburger on the table, bring her in, and if she starts for it, the second she starts for it, give her a sharp no. If she stops, praise her and give her a treat. Do this a couple of times."

"Okay."

"Then you have to see if she's learned. You leave her in the kitchen with the hamburger and watch."

"Ohhhhh!" I say. "What if she eats it?"

"You keep working on it. Counter surfing is not okay in any form. Food that drops on the floor—how is she with that?"

"I'm not sure."

"Drop something and see what she does. If she goes for it, stop it immediately. She's smart. She'll get the idea."

I'm picturing one of Maudie's pizzas on the counter; I'm not sure I would be able to walk away from that! It's not easy being a guide dog in training.

"She's good when we're walking. She doesn't stop the way she used to."

"You're doing fine. There are a lot of moving parts here."

Then I hear the news.

Next week the puppy club is going to do a puppy de-stress event at a local college. This involves, but is not limited to, a lot of students hugging Lumie, which I'm sure she'll love. Normally, she can't be petted when we're out in the world, but Brian says, "This is a meet and greet. We want the students to feel comfortable and for the dogs to play. We'll take the vests off the dogs so they won't be working. But Lumie's a little young. We'll keep an eye on her in case she gets overloaded."

I don't know, exactly, how stressed college students can get. I mean, school is just starting, but I guess they're all thinking ahead to finals already.

"We'll be there," I say. "Do I have to know anything special?"

Brian smiles. "You know anything about stress?"

"Absolutely."

"You'll ace it."

"LUMIE, WE'RE GOING to go help extremely stressed college students who are in the library worrying. They need you." I drop a small piece of cheese on the floor and she looks at me, then back at the cheese. "Leave it," I say.

She sighs. "Good girl!" I give her a treat and a massive hug.

The puppy club needs three cars to get us all to the college. I ride with Brian and his dog Bolder. Phil and Laney, two club members, pile in with their dogs, Misty and Mariah. With all these dogs, this is not a stress-free car!

Lumie sits on my lap, which she loves. "You know what you have to do today," I tell her as Brian pulls up to the college. "Be adorable. That's one of your specialties."

I don't know my way around this school, but Brian, Phil, and Laney have been here before. The guard at the library door kneels down and pets Bolder. Then he walks us through the door and down the hall as Brian reminds us, "If any of the students seem nervous around dogs, be respectful of that."

We stop. All the raisers from the club are here. We remove the vests from the dogs. "Shake it off," Brian says. The older dogs know this means they're not working today.

Lumie is just happy to be here. Two students see the dogs and make the noise.

"Ohhhhhhhhhhhhh!"

We are walking through the library now, a dog parade; one girl looks up, stands up, and raises her hands. Another gets on her knees as a dog comes right up to her. This huge guy comes over to Lumie, sits on the floor, and says, "Hey, small dog." Lumie puts her paw on his knee.

"That means she likes you," I tell him.

He gives her the biggest hug and says he's from Texas and he misses his dog so much. Lumie does a stand-in for his dog and she gets rubbed and hugged. A few more students come over.

"Hi, baby. I need you. Can you come live in my dorm?"

Lumie looks at me and I shake my head.

A nervous boy stands by the wall, his hands in his pockets. I want to tell him, Don't be afraid, but I just smile at him.

And now it's a pileup of stressed students and a pile-up of non-stressed dogs who are giving their happiness to everyone who gets close. I give Lumie a treat and tell her, "Good girl," but she already knows she's a good girl, since about nineteen students are telling her that at once. I wonder if I need to pull her out, if it's too much. She's not whimpering or backing away; her tail isn't between her legs. These are all the things Brian said to look for. She just cuddles up to this one shy girl in the corner, who I can see really needs to hug a puppy. This girl buries her face in Lumie's fur.

"This seems like a good school," I tell her.

"I hope so," she says quietly.

"They understand about dogs here," I say. "That's a good school."

She laughs. "You're right!" I see her sit up and smile and now she's talking to another girl behind her.

Yes, we are cutting through the stress of this place! We are making a difference!

Lumie makes a tiny whine like she has to go.

Kids are surrounding her and it's hard for me to get her out. The nervous boy who was standing by the wall comes over now and reaches out his hand to scratch her head.

Too late.

Here, in the library, by the checkout desk, on the blue rug, she pees.

"I'm so sorry!" I say, and the librarian is actually laughing, which I'm glad about. All the students are laughing too.

"It's fine," the librarian says.

Brian makes a face at me, like I should have been more careful. Brian not being happy with me, I've got to tell you, is tough.

"I'm sorry," I tell him. "I got a little confused."

"It happens." He hands me paper towels and a bottle of pee-and-poop spray to take away the smell.

"I'm really sorry, Brian." I'm looking for some kind of smile from him while I blot up the accident.

"It happens."

Here I am at this de-stress event and I feel the stress rising up from my toes and into my stomach.

I should have been more careful. I could see she needed to go out.

On the way home in the car I tell him, "I won't make that mistake ever again."

"You'll probably make more mistakes, Olive," he says to me. "We all do."

But Lumie is the best of the best. I want to be that too.

"You helped a lot of people today," Brian tells me. "Focus on that."

Olive's Rules on Helping

1. Pretty much, it's always a good time to help somebody.
2. Small things like smiles can make a big difference.
3. Show up with a puppy—you can't lose.

25

Dangers

THE SMELL OF HAMBURGER is everywhere in the kitchen.

"This, Lumie, is your ultimate test."

Lumie looks right up at me, sniffing the hamburger.

I tell her, "We're going to practice saying no to hamburger, and after you get this down, we're going to see if we can get Maudie off of ice cream." Maudie has been on a major ice cream binge since she broke up with Roger.

I finish frying a hamburger in a pan. "This is not for you, Lumie."

She looks up at me like I am the source of all things. There is a special light in her eyes that comes from a deep place.

I put the burger on a plastic plate, put the plate on the counter, and say, "Lumie, come."

Lumie gazes up at the burger.

She sighs deeply.

"No! Lumie, come!"

She turns from the burger and walks to me.

"Good girl!" I give her a treat. "Organic turkey pellets. Yum."

She looks back at the burger.

"Not for you," I say, and give her another treat.

LUMIE IS PLAYING with her ball in the backyard. She is totally focused on this ball, and after I throw it to her about a hundred times, the game, at least for a human, gets a little boring. Miss Nyla is watering her flowers.

I say, "They're beautiful, Miss Nyla."

"Thank you, dear. This garden is my joy."

"My mom grew sunflowers."

"Did she?" She looks across the garden. "We need sunflowers here. Those flowers have attitude. Would you help me plant them?"

"Oh, yes, ma'am."

I roll the ball farther—Lumie pounces, but it keeps rolling.

"Go get it, girl!"

She races after it, her little tail up.

That's when I see it.

A huge raccoon, making strange noises. This animal looks confused.

"Lumie!" I try not to shout. "Come. . . ."

The raccoon looks like something's wrong with it and it's heading right for Lumie, moving slow, like its legs aren't working well. I race to get her, but Lumie thinks we're playing, and runs farther away. I can't get past the raccoon to get to her.

"Lumie. Come. Come to me."

Lumie doesn't move.

The raccoon is creeping toward her. I'm desperately looking for something to throw at it. A rake! I grab it, shout, "Get out!" But Lumie's so close, I might hit her.

"Miss Nyla, use your hose!"

She turns, sees the situation. Her old face gets hard.

"Lumie," I say with as much confidence as I've got, "come."

Miss Nyla turns the nozzle and out comes a power

spray that scares that raccoon up over the fence and across the next yard until I can't see it anymore.

"Awesome!" I shout. I drop the rake and race to Lumie.

"It's okay, girl." I'm trying not to cry. I pick her up. "It's okay. It's okay." I bury my face in her soft fur.

Miss Nyla walks over and puts her arm around my shoulder. "She'll be fine."

I'm shaking. The dog is calm. "You saved her, Miss Nyla."

She grins. "I'd say we worked as a team."

Lumie leans into me and looks up, which is exactly what she's supposed to do. "You've got to come when I tell you. It's not a suggestion."

I'm going to have to tell Brian this happened.

Between the raccoon and the big pee in the library, I'm figuring I get an F- in puppy raising this week.

I hope Brian doesn't lose faith in me.

BRIAN COMES OVER an hour after I call him. I say, "In all the things you gave me to read, I don't remember anything about raccoons."

Brian is looking at Lumie's face. "You're right about the raccoons—we should add something. They can be nasty." He holds Lumie up, who is trying to lick his ear. "How you doing, little one?"

Lumie wags her tail and acts like nothing happened.

Me, I'm a mess. My heart is beating fast; I'm trying to breathe normally.

Brian smiles. "I'd say you took the trauma for her, Olive. This puppy is fine."

"Does that mean you're not upset with me?"

Brian looks at me strangely. "Why would I be upset?"

Maybe I shouldn't remind him. . . .

Miss Nyla is standing behind Brian, shaking her head like I should shut up now.

Brian hands Lumie back to me. "Being a good raiser doesn't mean difficult things won't ever happen—some dogs get sick, they get bad allergies. Just yesterday one of our adult guide dogs, Donavan, was attacked by a neighbor's dog."

"Is Donavan going to be okay?" I shout. I look down at Lumie, who is looking up at me.

"Yes. He's a tough one. And you're doing fine, Olive. More than fine."

I nod desperately. "Right." I put my hands over my mouth and breath in and out slowly. A paper bag would be better, but Brian doesn't know I have panic attacks.

I'd like to keep it that way.

Attacking raccoons, stressed-out college students, bad boyfriends.

Just another week in the life of Olive Hudson, puppy raiser.

I put Lumie in her crate with a chew toy, flop on the couch, and have a meltdown—not a huge one, but still.

26

Jordan

JORDAN HAS DELAYED giving his leadership oral report for as long as he can.

I've offered to listen, to even listen in another room so he doesn't have to look at me, but he doesn't want to do that. His mother made him practice the speech in front of her and she kept telling him to slow down.

"Did you write it all out?" I ask.

"Of course I did!"

"Do you want me to read it?"

"No."

"Do you want me to stop asking if I can help?"

"Yes."

"I think you're going to ace it, Jordan."

He makes a noise and adjusts his new black-frame glasses on his nose. "I changed the end," he says.

"Well, ends are hard."

He scratches Lumie's head and walks off fast.

How can he walk so fast when he can't see too well? Maybe those glasses are helping.

"Jordan!" I run after him. "If I ask you something, you don't have to say yes or be polite."

"Okay, I'll be rude."

I ask fast: "I've been wondering if I could come and hear your speech."

Jordan takes off his glasses, rubs his eyes, and doesn't say anything.

"I'd be super quiet. And, if you want, you could bring Lumie on the stage with you."

"It isn't a stage; it's a platform."

"I think she'd be okay on a platform."

Lumie looks at me and at Jordan as he puts his glasses back on. "You don't have to, Olive."

"I know. Should I sit in the front or the back?"

"Sit next to my mother and make sure she doesn't get weird."

• • •

I AM SITTING in the middle of a big room with a banner that reads: YOUTH LEADERSHIP CONFERENCE. I'm sitting up straight to seem like a leader even though I haven't been trained.

Jordan is halfway through his presentation and right now he is talking fast. He speeds up and slows down. Twice his posters of guide dog puppies dropped on the floor. His mother sits next to me, clutching her necklace like she's watching a horror movie.

It's actually not that bad.

Lumie is up there with him and she's being such a good girl—I'm totally proud. I check my watch—four more minutes and he's done.

That's when something happens.

Jordan steps away from his posters and walks to the front of the platform. Lumie follows him on the leash.

His mother whispers, "What is he doing?"

Please don't do anything weird, Mrs. Feingold.

Jordan takes a huge breath as he looks out at all the kid leaders in the audience. He's holding Lumie's leash like it's the thing that's connecting him to courage.

"I want to end my presentation this morning by being pretty personal," he says. "There are so many visually impaired people I admire. But Morris Frank is one of my heroes. He helped cofound The Seeing Eye in 1929. Back then, blind people were treated differently than they are today. So many people told Morris Frank, you're blind, you can't do that. But he was the kind of person who said, 'Of course I can.' He had the first guide dog in America, Buddy. And together, they opened the way for guide dogs and their owners to be accepted all around the world. Morris Frank was all about bringing dignity and freedom to the blind. This is personal for me because I have some problems with my vision."

Mrs. Feingold is dabbing her eyes with a tissue.

"Things might get worse for me," Jordan says, "or they might not. But whichever way it goes, it's not going to stop me. No way." He smiles. "Working with guide dog puppies has ruined me for ever giving up."

Jordan steps back a little and Lumie does too. He backs up another step and, oh no!, he knocks his posters off the stand again. He starts laughing. "That happened because I'm nervous, not because of my eyesight!"

We all laugh too. Mrs. Feingold clasps her hands and says, "Ohhhh!"

He says, "I think I'm done. Thank you."

Everyone in the room stands and applauds as he picks things up.

But Lumie doesn't like the applause. She's pulling back a little. Jordan sees this and quiets everyone down.

The director of the program comes over and shakes his hand. I head to the front to get Lumie out of the room. Jordan grins and hands me her leash.

"Awesome," I tell him.

I do my confident power walk toward the door. Lumie follows alongside.

"You're a leader, Lumie. You know that?"

Maybe someday I can be a leader too.

27

School

HOW CAN IT be September already?

Lumie is seventeen weeks old, has all her vaccinations, and this means she can go anywhere.

But September means seventh grade is starting soon.

I don't know how I'm going to do it all.

Maudie and I go to the Three Bridges Middle School to register me and meet the principal. Bringing Lumie is a genius move too, because Dr. Eddington, the principal, wants to know everything about her and me. I show her how great Lumie is on the leash, which is a mistake, because Dr. Eddington wants to know something else.

"I would just love it, Olive, if you and Lumie would

do an assembly for the middle school about raising guide dog puppies."

I look at Maudie, who says, "That sounds like a great way for everyone to get to know Olive and the GDC."

I was hoping I could get to know people in small groups!

"I think our students would love meeting you and Lumie," the principal says. "And perhaps Jordan Feingold could be part of it too. He's one of our eighth graders. Do you know him?"

"We're friends. I'll have to check with the center, because they are in charge of what the puppies can and can't do."

"I understand."

She walks us around the school and takes us into the auditorium. "We seat six hundred," she explains.

I gulp. "At once?"

"Yes, Olive."

I look at Maudie, who raises both eyebrows, which is her Stay Calm expression. No way am I doing an assembly with six hundred kids!

My biggest concern is how Maudie is going to take care of Lumie while I'm at this school all day. I put together a list of questions for her to think about and I was shocked when she said I was overdoing it.

It wasn't that big a list.

1. Are you willing and able to give your full attention to Lumie throughout your workday?

2. Will you have one place for her to relieve herself near the office and make sure that she goes out regularly so she won't have an accident?

3. Do you fully commit to giving her one big walk at lunch, which will probably mean that you will need to eat lunch at your desk?

4. Do you promise that you will write down everything she does and report back to me on a regular basis?

5. Will you have cuddle times even if you are so busy you can hardly see straight?

6. Will you protect her from harm at all times?

7. Will you be on the lookout for people who will want to treat her like a pet?

8. Will you make sure that she eats only her official snacks from the Guide Dog Center?

9. Will you provide fresh water for her throughout the day?

10. Will you allow her to sit at your desk when you are working and take her with you to any meetings?

11. Will you memorize the small speech I've included so that when you have her out in public and people ask about her and the program, you can give them a good explanation?

12. Will you take her to the vet at the first sign of illness or distress?

Honestly, I don't think that's overdoing!

Think of all the people in the world who under-do and get nothing done!

And when I gave Maudie a simple report to fill out—a report that I made myself to make things easier for her, a report that I would need to receive by the end of each day—well, she looked at it and made a nasty face, and believe me, Maudie can make a seriously nasty face.

She said, "I'm not going to fill this out every day."

"Why not?"

"Because it's not required. You're being overbearing, Olive."

Overbearing?

I know all about this. We talked about it in sixth-grade life skills. I don't appreciate being insulted by a vocab word!

Well, I am ready to throw up from stress, because all this time I thought I could count on Maudie, who has done so much for me, and all I am asking is that she would do that much for Lumie.

But she won't commit to doing the kind of job that Lumie needs!

How can I go to school?

How can I function?

"Olive," Maudie says. "Relax."

I grip the arms of the chair I'm sitting on.

"Olive, it's going to be fine."

I say, "Following that list will make it be fine."

She sits across from me. "Look. You can have all the plans and points to follow in the world, but at the end of the day, you know what? People don't do things perfectly."

Maudie then says she has read all the rules from the GDC and she is going to do her best.

I was so upset that it didn't occur to me to thank her. If Maudie hadn't said yes to this, Lumie couldn't be with us.

The night before school starts, I take Lumie on a walk. "Things are going to be a little different," I tell her,

"but I will be walking you twice a day and you will get to go to work at Brian's company, where you have lots of friends and will be loved and adored, but not as much as I love and adore you. Okay?"

Lumie looks up at me like I've taught her to do. Brian says I've done a great job getting her to focus on me as her major source of everything.

It's hard to give that up, I'll tell you.

And if I'm being totally honest, I'm hoping Maudie won't be better at this than me. I mean, Maudie could be one of those easy puppy raisers who lets a dog get away with things and the dog thinks they're terrific.

All right. I said it. In addition to being totally stressed, I'm potentially jealous.

This, trust me, is a terrible combination.

28

Happy Birthday, Dad

DAD'S BIRTHDAY IS tomorrow, September 3. Maudie and I are driving to Grandma's apartment, which is near our old house. We're going to celebrate his life together.

Dad loved country music, so we are bringing our guitars to sing.

He loved dogs, so we are bringing Lumie, who is sleeping in the back seat.

He loved, loved barbecue, so we are having a barbecue in his honor. Becca and her mom are coming.

And we are going to visit his grave.

I want to celebrate Dad, but I don't want to go to the cemetery.

Miss Nyla put together the most beautiful basket of

plants to put by his headstone. I haven't seen the head-stone yet.

It's supposed to rain tomorrow. If it rains really hard, maybe we shouldn't go.

I can't believe how much has changed since we left the house on Pleasant Street. We get to Grandma's and I hug her so hard, eventually she says, "Honey, I'm going to have to sit down."

She made gingerbread and lemonade. I don't know how she knew what we needed, but she did.

They were on the table. Two photo albums. "You want to do this chronologically or as the mood hits you?" Grandma asks me and Maudie. Her nurse, Charlotte, is leaving.

"I'll be back in the morning, Mrs. Hudson." Charlotte smiles at us. "You're in good hands."

We have pizza delivered, the kind Dad always ordered—extra cheese with pepperoni.

Grandma lifts the blue album and says, "Let's begin at the beginning. With you, Maudie. I don't make any claim to doing this right—I just chose a few photos that I love and I hope you do too."

Maudie bites her lip and nods for her to go ahead.

Grandma opens the album to a picture of Maudie as a little girl laughing her head off as she's chasing a butterfly. "You were two years old," Grandma says. "I took that photo at your parents' first house. Your mother had a butterfly garden. She loved them. Do you remember?"

I'm not sure Maudie does. "Well, whether you do or not, those butterflies are part of you." Maudie puts her hand over her mouth as Grandma turns to the next photo. This time Maudie is peering down from a tree and Dad is looking up at her. "Now, this one was your sixth birthday, and that tree was just about your favorite thing in the world. You could climb it like a squirrel—your father let you go too high, in my opinion. But there you go."

Dad's face is so loving and Maudie's face is so happy. She touches the photo. "I remember."

"It's good you do, because memory is important. Sometimes, I know, it stings and burns, but other times it's like pouring syrup on a spoon and just eating it."

The next three pictures are of Maudie standing at an easel and drawing. Her face is so focused. An older woman and man are smiling at her.

"Those were my grandparents, my mom's parents," she tells me. "They lived two blocks away from us. I visited them so often."

Grandma says, "You loved that midnight blue to color in a sky."

"I still do, Grandma. Did you take all these pictures?"
Grandma smiles. "I did."

"You're good," Maudie says.

We look through the others—Maudie with a fluffy kitten, Maudie with her mother—the two of them smiling bright.

Maudie studies this one. "I forgot about this day. I always loved this picture. Mom took me to the ballet." She looks up, smiling at Grandma. "And you were there waiting for us."

"Yes, I was."

The last photo Grandma has is of Maudie walking down a lawn wearing her graduation gown and throwing her hat in the air.

"Thank you," she tells Grandma. "These are good memories."

Grandma closes the blue book and pushes it toward her. "It's for you."

My album has the same number of photos—eight. There is one of me as a baby, crying as my mother holds me. Mom's face is lowered close to my little head, like she is trying to cover me with all her love. There is one of my dad lifting me way up in the air and we are both laughing while Mom watches. Then—here it is! The picture of

Maudie holding me when I was a baby. I'm really crying too, and Maudie just deals with my intense infant drama.

Here's another one of me and our dog, Bitsy, flopped on the lawn.

Me, at age six, seven, and eight sitting on the hood of Dad's plumbing van that was decorated with streamers for National Plumbers' Day.

Me and Dad playing guitars on the patio.

"Well," Grandma says, "eight pictures can just show so much, but both of you were . . . both of you are mighty strong despite some tough storms. I love you both so much."

LUMIE, BEING A GUIDE DOG PUPPY in training, can come to the cemetery. She only tries to pee once on a tree, but I think she knows something important is happening. Dad's headstone reads,

JOE HUDSON—

WHO LOVED LIFE RIGHT TO THE END

I can't look at it for long at first, but then I can.

Maudie sings the most beautiful song and plays her

guitar. I was going to play along with her, but I can't play and cry at the same time.

Becca's mom helps me plant Miss Nyla's flowers on Dad's grave. She holds Lumie close and puts a flower on the ground like she did at the funeral eight months ago.

It is beyond good to see Becca. We stay up talking until three in the morning.

She was with me when Dad got sick and when he died.

I was with her when her parents got divorced and her father married another woman one week later.

We make a list of all the moments we can remember. We make an extra copy and put it in the thick cream-colored envelopes Becca brought. We seal the envelopes.

Becca writes *Forever Friends* on each one. We sign our names and the date. Lumie sniffs both envelopes.

I don't eat much barbecue. I am filled up with other things.

On the way home I tell Maudie, "I feel like a camel who just got extra water inside for the next part of the journey."

29

The *Lumie News*

THE FIRST DAY of seventh grade.

I'm completely ready and Maudie is not. All I do is mention that she could take a video of Lumie and send it to me every day by noon so I can look at it at lunch.

"No," is what she says, and hugs me. "Have a great first day."

Mr. Burbank gets up early to say goodbye, like I'm his granddaughter. "You're looking strong. Go burn it up out there."

The bus driver, Mrs. Rover, is funny, especially when she shouts, "Have no doubt, children, who is in control!"

"We are!" one boy yells.

That's when Mrs. Rover pulls the bus to the side of the road and says in a voice of total authority, "Incorrect. Every second you're on this bus, I'm in charge. Any questions?"

Quiet descends, and the boy who shouted "We are!" slumps in his seat.

The first-day-of-school icebreaker question is excellent:

What would you do if you won a million dollars?

I raise my hand and say, "I'd build a dog rescue center and have a swimming pool and a thousand acres so they could run around and have a good life."

We get into groups with kids who answered the question a little like we did, although no one answered like me. Maya Mercer is in my group. She said she would give the million dollars to help homelessness.

Despite all this, I am having trouble concentrating. I'm working hard to not be worried about Lumie.

Maya and I have lunch together and during lunch, the only time you're allowed to use your phone at this school, the only time you can even touch it, I get this from Maudie.

THE *LUMIE NEWS*—FIRST EDITION

by Maudie A. Hudson,
publisher and editor at large

Updated 12:17 ET, Tuesday, September 6

Lumie arrived at goodWorks in excellent spirits.
She spent time with Marshall, an eight-week-old
   puppy, who tried to ride on her back, but
   Marshall quickly learned that was a bad idea.
Lumie was able to assist Maudie twice in not
   giving up on the "Happiness" campaign.
A proper poop place has been established and as
   of this writing Lumie is sitting under Maudie's
   desk chewing a rubber chicken into oblivion.
Christine will be walking Lumie at 2 p.m., and
   Christine doesn't mess around.

I lean back, grinning.
"What?" Maya says.
I show Maya sixty-three recent photos of Lumie to get
her ready for the *Lumie News* and Maya makes the noise.
"Ohhhhhhhhhhhhhhhh!"

I show her the first edition that Maudie just sent.

Maya says, "You have a great big sister."

This is totally true.

IT'S SO GOOD to walk Lumie when I get home. She jumps in the air when she sees me, so I guess I wasn't forgotten. We race down the path behind the Stay Awhile.

It's like the birds are chirping just for us.

Like the sun is shining right on our personal path.

"Come on, girl. I need to get in shape for track."

Lumie is a good runner—she's fast, like me. We tear down the path, and I jump over a rock to show off. At the next rock, Lumie jumps over it.

"Good, girl!"

She wags her tail. I love how dogs show you instant appreciation. Some people, you wonder if they're paying attention, if they even care. Ellis, a boy in my homeroom, had to stand next to me in line, and he acted like it was the worst moment of his life. A major strength of dogs is that they just love being with you. One hundred percent.

We get to the end of the path, which ends at Brian's backyard. We turn around and I say, "Let's go home, girl!" We run fast and head for home.

That's when it hits me. This is the first time I've

thought of the Stay Awhile as home. The warmth of that soaks into me and I run faster to get there. Lumie runs alongside.

I think she feels it's home too.

Home for a while, for us both.

When I get home, Maudie is sitting on the porch reading *How to Raise a Terrific Teenager*. I'll be honest, this book makes me nervous.

What chapter is she on?

Is this book giving her good advice?

"Hi," I say, trying to look terrific, but Maudie is focusing on the book and doesn't see me. I look over her shoulder. One sentence sticks out.

> Remember, it's not that you fall; it's what you do next that counts.

I'm not sure if this is referring to the teenager falling or to the adult, but it seems to me that some things are obvious—like, if the teenager breaks her arm, the next thing you do is call the doctor. Right?

Maudie sees me now. "Hi."

"Hi."

Lumie squeaks hello.

Maudie underlines a sentence.

> Remember the tough times you've been
> through and how you climbed out.

"We've already done that," I say. "I think you can skip ahead."

She laughs and I do too. I sit on a step. Here I am. Me and my sister. My half sister. But there's something about that word *half* that doesn't feel complete, like saying, "All I have is half a cookie." I mention this issue of fractions to Maudie, who says sometimes half a thing is enough.

She says, "You can be half-crazy."

"Half-full," I add.

She giggles. "Half-baked. Half-hearted."

My turn. "You could eat half a sandwich at half speed."

Maudie thinks. "Or be a half cousin to a halfback—"

"With a half-dollar in your pocket staring up at a half-moon for a full half hour!"

"You win," she says.

We sit there not talking. We don't have to.

I don't know about Maudie, but I'm starting to feel whole.

● ● ●

"KID, I'M UP early here to impart wisdom. You're getting this for free."

I adjust my book bag and wait for Mr. Burbank to impart.

"My mother, may she rest in peace, told me, if you say a nice word to a mean person, it always throws them off."

Lumie sits, thinking about it.

"That's good, sir."

"You may go," he says.

On the bus, I tell Ellis to have a good day after he tells me that the entire school voted and no one wants me here.

Maya says, "He says that to every new kid, Olive."

In music with Mr. Paglia, I have to stand in front of Ellis in the chorus. But, strangely, he is silent, except for when the altos have to sing:

We will be there for you
We're your friends, we'll see you through

This is a good song we're learning—a song that can shut a mean kid up. Mr. Paglia is all over the place when he teaches, which is my favorite way to learn.

He tells us he used to sing opera, then throws back his head and sings this complicated song in Italian.

He introduces us to his clown fish, Pagliacci, who is named after a famous singing clown that I've never heard of. The fish twirls in his bowl as Mr. Paglia says, "I'm going to say the smartest thing about music, and then keep repeating it all year. Are you ready?"

Pagliacci waits. We do too.

"Everybody has music in them. Period. Don't let anything or anybody tell you otherwise. Am I a genius or what?"

Most of us agree he's a genius.

At lunch, Maya and I are waiting for it.

"Check your phone, Olive; maybe it's—"

I'm checking and there's nothing. But . . .

"Wait. Here it is."

THE *LUMIE NEWS*—SECOND EDITION

by Maudie A. Hudson,
publisher and editor at large

Updated 12:20 ET, Wednesday, September 7

Breaking News: Lumie greeted Brian's biggest
    customer by jumping on her and almost
    knocking her down. Christine said a sharp

no—Lumie sat instantly. Brian helped his
customer, who is a really good sport, to a chair
and gave her water.

Marshall showed Lumie his toy filled with treats
and Lumie ate every one, teaching Marshall
a valuable lesson.

Lumie is pleased with her poop place.

As of this writing Lumie is sleeping under
Maudie's chair with her head on Maudie's
left foot.

"She should send pictures," Maya says.

"She's doing what she can."

30

Homework

I MIGHT HAVE more people who want to help me with homework than I need. Mr. Burbank loves science, Lu Lu Pierce is anything reading, Miss Nyla is a math whiz, and Maudie knows how to present an idea.

I save the homework I'm most looking forward to for last. It's an essay for English titled "What I learned . . ."

Most everyone who knows me would think I'd write about dogs. Not tonight.

What I Learned Having a Plumber for a Father

1. I learned how things work.
2. I learned to like puzzles, because every

plumbing job is really a problem and you have to figure it out.

3. I learned that some jobs are done in secret—or at least no one will see the work when you're done. (This is a lot like raising a puppy, because no one will know all the hours I have put into helping Lumie, my guide dog in training).

4. I have learned that working with your hands and wanting to do the best by people is a very satisfying life.

5. I have learned to be good at some emergencies—and that people who are having emergencies need someone to walk through their door who is NOT having an emergency at that moment. That person can be you.

6. I have learned that a good tool kit has the basic tools I will need on most jobs, and I must keep it with me at all times.

7. I have learned that if you're good at what you do, your age doesn't matter.

8. I have learned the importance of good

posture when you walk into a home to help
someone, because if you're slouching and
looking down, you don't look like a person
who knows what they're doing. BUT, if you
walk straight and tall and you smile, well,
even if you're not quite sure what to do,
people will have confidence in you. And
somewhere in the universe when that
happens—all that confidence collides and
helps you do a great job. No kidding.

9. I have learned that doing a good job is one
   of life's great feelings, and doing a bad job
   never feels right.

I feel a massive surge of confidence about this first
piece of writing for English. I show it to Maudie, who
says, "Nice work."

On my way out the door the next morning I show it to
Mr. Burbank, who says it's got heart and grit, his favorite
combination.

I turn it in to Mrs. Tullerman with a huge smile and
the next day I get it back, with, I'm not kidding, an I for
"Incomplete"! And this:

These are excellent and innovative thoughts, Olive, and I love the way they tell us not just about what you learned, but about your father. However, this is not in essay format. It is a list. If you would like to rewrite it, and I suggest that you do, please follow the proper essay style that we discussed in class and then I will give you a grade.

I have every confidence you will excel in English this year. —Mrs. T

I've been at this school for forty-eight hours and I'm already incomplete! *Incomplete* is a throw-you-down-on-the-floor word. For two periods I decide that English is my most hated class and that Mrs. T has no heart. I hope Lumie is doing better than me. I need a dog to hug and the only animal at this school is a clown fish.

But by fifth-period study hall, I decide this:

No way am I going to let Dad's wisdom get an Incomplete!

Words pour out of me, but this time Dad's wisdom is coming as a poem, which is not an essay. When the words inside you are oozing out, it's hard to tell them to get into the right format. But I do.

Personal Essay by Olive Hudson, second draft

What I've Learned Having a Plumber for a Father

"If you take it apart, you've got to put it back together again, and I don't want any part left over."

Dad always told me that.

The first thing I remember taking apart was the toaster, but that didn't go so well. I just paid attention to unscrewing everything and didn't think about what it would look like to put the parts back together. When Dad got home from work, I was sitting on the kitchen floor with fifty pieces of a toaster on newspaper. At least I thought of newspaper.

Dad looked at the mess and before he could say anything, I jumped in. "How much do you like this toaster?"

"How much *did* I like it," he said. "We are definitely dealing in past tense here."

My dad wanted me to know how things worked. He was a plumber and he always told me that every plumbing job is like a puzzle and you have to figure it out. He showed me that working with your hands and wanting to do the best by people is a very satisfying life.

Plumbing is one of those jobs that people don't understand. When you're a plumber, most of the jobs you do won't be seen by other people. Pipes are behind walls, under sinks, in the ceiling. It's secret work. And that taught me that what matters is how good your work is, not that people see it. My dad always said, "Doing a good job is one of life's great feelings, and doing a bad job never feels right."

One of my dad's specialties was handling emergencies. He did this with skill and good posture, since no one is going to have confidence in a slouching plumber coming into their house. I suppose there were a million other things he told me about life, and many of those lessons are written across my heart, which is why they will never receive a grade, and I'm okay with that.

Mostly, my dad taught me the importance of being a true person. I'm sure that's why he won New Jersey's coveted Good Guy plumber award three years in a row.

I do a double check on spelling and punctuation.

Okay, Mrs. T, it's up to you to do the right thing and love this.

31

Brave

I GET AN A.

Mrs. T wrote, *Olive, well done. Keen observations, good use of dialogue and memory. I hope to meet your father.*

I close my eyes.

You'll like my sister, Mrs. T. I swear.

THE *LUMIE NEWS* dedicates the next few weeks to headline news:

**LUMIE LEARNS TO WALK DOWN
A STEEL STAIRCASE.**

LUMIE TRIES TO EAT A SHOPPING CART.

Note from me: there was no explanation on the shopping cart incident and you can imagine what I was thinking!

LUMIE RIPS INTO MAUDIE'S LAST BOX OF STRAWBERRY DOUBLE-FROSTED POP-TARTS

By this time, *Lumie News* is trending at Three Bridges Middle School. For a new kid, I am known by just about everybody. Kids are always trying to sit with me and Maya at lunch and in the halls. Everyone wants to know what Lumie is up to. Dr. Eddington comes up to me and says, "I'm still hoping we can have you and someone from the GDC do an assembly, Olive."

I nod, and think about that huge stage. Every time we have an assembly, I picture myself on that stage, terrified, unable to speak, everyone laughing, Lumie looking up at me, thinking, Why have you brought me here?

LUMIE'S NEW SMELL OF THE DAY IS A SKUNK.

What??????

Assorted kids scream, "What?????" in the hallway.

I finally get the inside story. It turns out the skunk had bad aim. He missed Lumie and got a squirrel, who is now beyond miserable.

It also turns out that Maudie has to visit her mother, but that did not make the headline news.

"She's not doing so well," Maudie says without any of her normal energy. "She's . . . well . . . sick."

"I'm sorry. What kind of sick?"

What a stupid thing I just said. Maudie looks sad and I say "I'm sorry" again.

"She's been sick for a long time."

"Oh." I don't understand any of this. "I'm sorry."

"You don't have to keep saying you're sorry."

"Sorry."

And now I see Maudie do something I've seen her do only once before—at Dad's funeral—cry.

"I'm fine," she says.

Not at this exact instant you're not.

I sit next to her, hoping she'll tell me more. I put my arm around her shoulders as Lumie trots up with her special brand of love.

Maudie sniffs. "Thanks, girl." Lumie lays her head in Maudie's lap. "She's not dying, Olive. It's not that."

"That's good."

"She's sick in a different way."

I nod like I get it. I sure don't.

"I guess it's more like she's stuck. She can't let go of the past. She's angry. She has a lot of hate. She forgot how to love people." Maudie lowers her head. "And sometimes it spills over."

"You're so not like that, Maudie."

"Thanks."

Lumie looks up at her in complete agreement.

"I don't want to go," Maudie says. "It's hard to be with her."

"I can go with you."

"Thanks, but no—"

"Seriously. Lumie and I can come."

"Wouldn't work."

"She doesn't like me?"

"She doesn't know you. She hates Dad."

Part of me doesn't want to hear any more, but the other part says, *Listen*.

"She blamed him for everything. She said I couldn't see him."

That's why Maudie didn't come around.

"I stayed away from him. I didn't believe everything

she said, but I didn't know what to do. And she kept getting worse."

She must hate it that we're living together.

"I won't stay long—just a day. Christine said you can stay at her house."

"Do you want to bring Lumie?"

"She should stay with you." Maudie gets up and dries her face with a towel.

"I think you're brave," I say.

Maudie smiles sadly. "You're right. I am." She starts packing.

The next day Maudie's mother calls and says, don't come.

Maudie unpacks. I don't know what to say.

"She does this when her depression gets bad," Maudie tells me. "I used to ignore that and go to her house to help, but the last time I did that, she wouldn't answer the door. I could see her sitting in the living room and she wouldn't answer the door."

"Was she like that when she and Dad were married?"

"No. Not at all."

32

Assembly

THE TREES ARE changing color, especially the big oak in front of the Stay Awhile, thick with yellow leaves. Lu Lu Pierce says, "That old thing's showing off."

In a few weeks, it starts dropping its leaves.

The *Lumie News* is still going strong.

Parent-teacher conferences begin. I tell Maudie, "You don't have to go, since you're not my parent."

"Nice try," she says.

"The teachers might not take you seriously—I mean, a sister isn't as big a force as, say, a father."

Maudie stands. I look way up at her. "You can go," I tell her.

It turns out the teachers like me. It also turns out that Dr. Eddington really wants an assembly on raising guide dog puppies.

Brian says, "Lumie's old enough to handle it."

Jordan promises he'll support me from the audience. "Remember, Olive. Knowing how to be a leader is knowing how to give a speech without puking onstage."

I feel like at any minute I could throw up.

I give Lumie a bath so she'll be extra adorable.

Maudie will be with me onstage along with Brian and Christine—all tall people I can hide behind if necessary.

And Maudie says the best thing to me.

"You don't have to talk in the assembly if you don't want to. Do the thing you're best at."

"That's okay?"

"Yes."

Well, that changes most everything, and I realize that walking onstage with Lumie in her vest and getting her to stand there with me isn't too scary. Getting her to sit when I sit, and then walking up and down the aisles of the auditorium so kids can see her, but not pet her because she's working—hey. I can do that.

A woman, Evelyn, who is visually impaired, talks about how much having a dog means to her.

Just as she starts to talk, Lumie does her I-need-to-pee whine.

Are you serious? You went right before we entered the school.

Another whine.

One thing I know for sure—there is absolutely no peeing allowed in the assembly.

Brian signals for me to take care of it, although I'm not sure how to leave. Then he raises his hand and says, "Sorry to interrupt, but, Evelyn, we have to take Lumie outside for a minute."

Most everyone in assembly knows what that's about and there's a lot of laughing as Lumie and I rush out the auditorium and head down the hall to the front door.

"She needs a bush," I tell the security guard, who smiles and lets me take Lumie outside. "Okay, Lumie, go here."

She does and looks relieved that we're not in that huge auditorium right now.

"You're so good with all those people, Lumie. Everyone loves you. And me, I'm so proud."

I would like to just stay by this bush and let the adults finish, but Lumie is the star. We walk back into the school, head past the sports awards in the glass case, and walk through the big double doors of the auditorium. All the kids, it seems, turn to look at us. I think I should have gone in the side entrance, but there's nothing to do now except walk down the middle aisle with total confidence like I do this every day of my life. It's good I've been practicing power walking.

My throat closes up, but I manage to say,

"Lumie, heel."

Jordan leads the assembly in silent applause—clapping hands in the air and not exactly touching.

And perfectly, like we've practiced, with six hundred faces looking right at us, we walk down the aisle, smiling at the kids we know, but mostly looking at the people we trust on the stage. Maudie and Brian and Christine.

Dr. Eddington stands up and says, "Olive, would you like to tell us a little about your experience raising Lumie?"

No, I wouldn't.

But I do.

I step up on the stage and Lumie stands next to me. "Sit," I tell her, and she does. "Good dog."

The kids appreciate how obedient she is, but that's not enough to make me not nervous.

Mr. Burbank told me, "When you're onstage and feeling nervous, picture everyone in the audience with a rabbit on their head and you'll lighten up."

I do that and start laughing.

"I just want to tell you all that when you raise a guide dog puppy, there's a special thing you get. You get to be part of that dog's life forever. Whatever the dog does, whoever the dog works with and helps and guides in the future, you've had a place in the dog's life when they were young. So if any of you are interested in being raisers, you can see me or Jordan after the assembly and we'll talk to you about it."

Silent applause again.

I just spoke in front of six hundred kids and did not die.

I back away from the mic, but then someone shouts.

"Hold old is Lumie?"

I smile. "Six months old today."

More silent applause.

After the assembly, forty-eight kids come up to learn about being a raiser.

Jordan and I say together, "It's the absolute best."

33

Too Fast

TODAY IS JANUARY 4—the anniversary of Dad's death.

The box came from the Biodegradable Balloon Company. We ordered six WE LOVE YOU, DAD! balloons to release into the sky in his memory. Maudie has a small helium tank that Lu Lu Pierce used in the library. Mr. Burbank holds Bunster. Miss Nyla walks down the stairs to watch. It's snowing a little outside. Lumie sniffs the box I'm opening and backs off when I shout, "Oh no!"

I lift out six silver balloons that read: WE LOVE YOU, AUNT EDNA!

"Everything," I shriek, "is ruined!"

Maudie looks at the balloons for a long time and finally says, "I'll be right back."

Mr. Burbank says, "Imagine what Aunt Edna's people got in their box."

I don't care about Aunt Edna or her people. This was supposed to be a major moment to honor Dad!

Maudie comes back down with her art supplies. She fills six balloons with helium and I tie a ribbon around them. Then Maudie takes a balloon and starts drawing a design around the AUNT EDNA letters. The design is so perfect, you can't see that anything was ever wrong. She paints DAD in big block letters. She does this on the second balloon, and on the next three.

Great art changes everything!

I hand her the last balloon and Maudie smiles. "Let's remember Aunt Edna."

We put our winter coats on and walk outside. A few snowflakes fall down.

"One, two, three . . ."

We let the balloons go. Maudie takes a picture.

I stand with Lumie and whisper, "I love you, Dad," as the balloons fly up to heaven.

• • •

LUMIE IS GROWING so fast. I wish she'd slow down, but I don't want to hold her back. It's like she knows she's got a big job to do. She loves putting on her green vest; she loves the times she's working.

Maudie is doing so well at goodWorks. She got a raise for the new campaign she created for their client Pencil Pals.

"A good ad should make you stop, look, and think," she said.

Maudie's been saving money like crazy so we can get out of debt. Each month when she pays off a bill, she rings a bell, and my job is to shout, "Yes!"

Lumie is now a year old. Jordan says the difference between a six-month-old puppy and a one-year-old dog is like the difference between a seventh grader and an eighth grader.

I'm not in eighth grade yet, since it's May. One more month in seventh grade, then we take the mountain.

Maudie made her mother a beautiful Mother's Day card with blues, purples, and greens—a gold heart is in the middle. Any mother would love that—I hope Maudie's mother will. After everything that's happened, Maudie still wants her mom to know she cares. Three days later on the actual Mother's Day, we get out our guitars.

"I've got a melody in my head," I tell her. I do a pick/strum, pick/strum on an Fm/C chord combination . . . and sing,

> *When two halves come together*
> *They make a whole*
> *They work it out together*
> *'Cause that's their goal*

Maudie makes up the middle part:

> *A whole is bigger*
> *A whole is stronger*
> *A whole is wonderful to see*

Me now:

> *That's what's happened*
> *For you and for me*

Good song! We keep singing it and I think Lumie is moving to the beat.

When two halves come together
They make a whole
They work it out together
'Cause that's their goal
A whole is bigger
A whole is stronger
A whole is wonderful to see
That's what's happened
For you and for me

MAY GIVES WAY to June and two days before seventh grade is over, Brian calls.

"They want to test Lumie soon," he says.

I'm not ready. But I have to be.

I know I've got . . .

Experience—check
Courage—check
Hope—double check
Stress—WOW—yes!
Sadness—yeah, I've got that. Check.
Pride—triple check

You should see Lumie. I don't think you'd recognize her.
She weighs fifty-one pounds.
All muscle. All heart.
This year, her growth has been amazing.
Mine too.
I don't know how I'm going to say goodbye.

34

Suddenly

IT'S JUNE 15. School ended yesterday.

Jordan just told me the best news: "I saw my new eye doctor, Olive, and he said my eyes haven't gotten worse."

"That's great!"

Maudie, me, Jordan, Lumie, and Omni, a guide dog puppy that Jordan is watching this weekend, are headed to the park for a walk before the party at Christine's house for Brian's birthday. The dogs are at our sides.

People smile as we walk by. It's an awesome feeling to have a guide dog in training.

We get to the front end of the park and a man asks, "You kids raise those dogs?"

"Yessir."

"Good for you," he says. Jordan tells the man about the GDC and I tell him, "It takes dozens of volunteers to support and train a guide dog. We're just one part of that."

Jordan hands him a brochure about the center. The man heads off. Maudie sees a friend from work and goes over to say hi. I kneel down and tie my shoe as Lumie sniffs the ground, going as far as the leash will—

A whoosh.

A growl.

The leash snaps tight.

Lumie cries out. I look up.

"Stop!" I shriek. "Stop!"

A fierce dog is attacking her!

It's got her at the neck. I try to reach her collar to pull her away.

"Stop it!" I shout.

"Call the police!" someone hollers.

The dog has Lumie on the ground and bites her stomach, but she's fighting back.

"No!" Jordan throws a big stick to stop it.

Everywhere people are shouting. Maudie runs up and kicks the attacking dog, who jumps up and bites her arm. Two men race to help.

"Back away!" the man shouts at the dog. "Back. Away!"

Someone throws a baseball at the attack dog. The dog jumps back. That gets Lumie free.

She can't walk. She's crawling, crying. I run to her.

"Olive, no!"

There's just enough room for Maudie to pick up Lumie. She has her in her arms like a baby, and we race out of the park.

Lumie's leg bone is sticking out of her fur. Her stomach is bleeding.

Maudie is running like a machine, even though her arm is bleeding.

I'm not sure I can keep up with her. I'm shaking, shouting, "It's okay. It's okay!"

One more block. Here's the animal hospital.

We run to the desk.

"We need help!" Maudie shouts. Lumie is still.

"Please!" I shout.

"The doctor's with—"

"Please!" Maudie says. And a doctor in a white coat comes out.

"In here," he says.

We lay Lumie on the table.

"It's okay, girl." But I don't think it's ever going to be okay.

The vet examines her. "She's still breathing. Her heart is strong. Her left rear leg is broken."

"This other dog attacked her," I try to explain, but I can't talk anymore.

He feels around her stomach, which is covered in blood, and shakes his head. "I don't know if—"

Don't say that!

A female vet comes in. "Let me take a look. Okay, good dog. Yes, you're a good dog. You had a day, huh? Let me see this. . . . Yeah . . . That hurts. . . . I know. She's going to need surgery. We need to take her upstairs."

I'm crying. "I have to go with her."

"You can't. I'm sorry."

She turns to Maudie. "Get that arm looked at right away."

A man gives Maudie a towel to put around the bleeding. "There's a hospital two blocks down."

Maudie says, "Olive, we have to let them do their job."

35

We're All Here

I tell my heart, be quiet

I tell my breath, you don't know it, but you can breathe

I tell my head, you don't know what's going to happen,
    so don't make it up

I tell my stomach, don't get sick, this is not the time

I tell my hands, stop shaking

I tell my ears, listen, just listen

I tell myself, not now, but soon, you're going to know

Remember what they said

Her heart is strong

Remember what you know

She's the best dog anywhere

Remember she's tough and you are too

And your sister, your colossal sister
She's close to a superhero
Close?
I think she's always been one

I wrote that sitting in the emergency room. Maudie gets a big bandage on her right arm and a rabies shot. The doctor says she'll have to have three more shots. Maudie shakes her head. "I don't need this right now."

"I think it's good they want to be careful, Maudie!"

Nothing can happen to you. Ever.

Brian is sitting in the waiting room with Jordan as we come out of the ER.

"Lumie's still in surgery," Brian says.

I nod and look down.

I should have been watching more.

I should have seen that dog running toward her!

We head over to the animal hospital, where the same man is at the desk.

"I can call up and see how she is," he says.

I can't quite talk.

He calls; Lumie is still in surgery.

We sit and wait.

I hate waiting.

Brian doesn't ask what happened.

He doesn't once say he has to go back to his barbecue.

Jordan looks at me. "It's not your fault."

"I didn't protect her."

"I was there, Olive. It's not anybody's fault."

THE SURGEON, DR. ROSARIO, comes out smiling. At least I think she's smiling; it's more like half a smile.

She walks toward me and Maudie. I stand up.

"Lumie's going to be okay."

I feel like a hundred pounds just dropped off of me.

"You've got one strong dog there."

"I know."

"She's got some healing to do—her back leg was broken. We set it and we closed the wound around her stomach."

That sounds like a lot. "Okay."

This doctor is smiling big now. "And do you know what? Her guide dog vest protected her neck. There were bite marks on the vest, but the attacking dog's teeth didn't go through."

Brian shakes his head; I don't have words, but I do hug this vet.

"We'll have to keep her overnight, maybe for two

nights, and then your own vet can see her."

"Can I see her?" I ask. "I'm the person she looks to."

The doctor puts her lips together tight and I think that means no. "We don't normally do that."

Maudie says, "But maybe this time . . . ?"

I'm thinking the four of us could wear the doctor down.

The doctor takes a big breath.

"I'm really good in hospitals," I say.

"She's in a crate. She's sleeping."

"I know what to do!"

The doctor looks at me.

"Please," I say. "I know what to do."

I HAVE TO WASH my hands like doctors do on television. I wear a yellow coat to be germ-free.

Lumie is sleeping in a crate on soft blankets. She has a bandage on her leg and one around her stomach. She's wearing one of those awful cones around her neck. I don't know how she can sleep in it.

"The cone is so she doesn't chew her bandages," the doctor says.

I know.

"She probably won't wake up until the drugs wear off."

I know.

I sit next to the crate and just look at her.

I'm sorry, girl.

I'm so sorry.

"Hey," I say.

I can see her sleeping and breathing away.

"Hey, girl. We're all here for you."

She moves a little. I put my fingers through the crate and touch her leg—not the one that's bandaged. I can hardly reach it, but I stroke her fur.

"Good dog," I say. "Good girl."

She moves a little. She's waking up.

"I know you've been through a lot, Lumie, but it's going to be okay, because all the people who love you are here."

Her head moves to look at me. Contact!

"I'm here. And I'm not going anywhere. I love you, okay?"

And this dog looks at me and, I swear, her eyes have that special spark in them. Still. After all that's happened!

How can that be?

"So, they tell me you've got a broken leg and a big bandage on your stomach. But they tell me your heart is strong. I knew that already."

Dr. Rosario says, "I think visiting time is up for today, Olive."

I could sleep here, but I don't ask. And I sure don't say what I'm thinking. . . .

I looked away for just a minute.

I was tying my shoe.

I've been careful of everything, except this.

I was always scared I was going to mess up and Lumie couldn't be in the program.

I failed the best dog ever.

I failed my friends and the program.

My mind and heart are tangled up, choking my thoughts.

I can't ask the question—will she be able to stay in the program?

I know the answer.

No.

No way.

Dr. Rosario doesn't know about the thought war going on in my head. "Don't worry, Olive. We're going to watch her. All her signs are strong."

"Thank you for everything." I walk slowly, so slowly to the door, trying to squeeze out every last minute. "I'll see you soon, Lumie. You're super strong, girl. Remember that."

It's impossible to walk slower than I'm doing without falling over. I'm at the door. Dr. Rosario walks out with me. "You know, I hear there's something quite wonderful happening in our waiting area."

"What?"

"I think you'll have to go down and see."

36

Champion

I RIDE THE elevator to the first floor. The door opens.

It's a party!

Lightning, Misty, and Mariah are right there like they're waiting for me. I'm not kidding!

Lightning and Misty run into the elevator.

"Wait, no!" I'm laughing and saying, "Out, come on, you can't stay in there!"

Now four other dogs from the puppy club surround me. I kneel down and try to hug each one, but this creates a major dog pile-on, which is exactly what I need!

Surrounded by dog love.

Now I notice the humans.

"What are you guys doing here?"

"Where else would we be?" That's Christine. She's eating chicken.

My keen sense of smell picks up the scent of important food. On a tall table is barbecued chicken, corn on the cob, fruit salad, and paw-print cupcakes.

Christine's daughter, Alexis, brings me a plate of food, which makes me even more popular with the seven dogs. I hold my plate high.

"No. Down. Good dog."

The raisers collect their dogs; the man at the front desk is eating and looking pretty happy.

Brian says to me, "I hear you were quite a hero in the park."

I shake my head. Not even close.

"It happened so fast," I tell him. "I didn't see anything until—"

"It's all right," Brian tells me.

Then I remember—this is Brian's birthday! He's having his birthday in a vet hospital! "I'm sorry about your party . . . " I begin.

Brian waves his hand, like, no big deal. "I've had a lot of them. Believe me. This location, though, is a first."

The puppy club wants to know about Lumie and I tell

them about how brave she was and how she recognized my voice and listened when I talked to her.

"I'm coming back first thing in the morning to sit with her until they throw me out." I smile. "It's so good to see you guys."

Puppy clubbers stay together.

I need to update my Who Has My Back list.

The dogs circle around me as Dr. Rosario comes out the elevator. Christine gives her barbecue; the dogs come up to her.

I walk over, grinning. "Welcome to the party."

"You live in a good world, Olive."

When seven dogs are at a party, you hear a different kind of conversation.

Good dog.

Down.

No. I said down.

Drop it.

Sit.

Good dog.

Very good dog.

Hey!

Time-out!

Brian is the king of time-outs. He pulls two dogs into different corners. "Easy," he says. The dogs settle down. I walk over.

Now Lu Lu and Miss Nyla walk through the door carrying cookies and behind them is Mr. Burbank with Bunster in a carry crate.

"How's the pup?" Mr. Burbank asks.

"She's sleeping. She's going to be okay."

"Of course she is." Mr. Burbank shoves a carrot stick in Bunster's crate and grabs a piece of chicken for himself. "She's a champion."

Remember that, Lumie.

Remember who you are.

37

Long Week

JORDAN KEPT CALLING the Animal Control hotline to see if they had captured the dog that attacked Lumie. Finally, they did! It was a guard dog who had escaped and was trained to attack.

Maudie said, "We're going to put that attack behind us."

We're all about moving forward in this family!

Becca sends me a picture of glowing candles in a church.

I lit candles for Lumie!

Lumie is coming home today and we have everything ready. We have towels and soft blankets. Jordan washed Lumie's crate and lined up all her toys so she could play with new ones during the day and not get bored.

I unroll my sleeping bag by her crate.

I tell Maudie, "This is where I'm going to sleep."

"For how long?"

"As long as I have to."

She doesn't tell me I can't. As a big sister, she is really coming along.

Brian comes to the hospital with us and carries Lumie out to our car. I've covered the back seat with towels and have a soft pillow for her to lie on.

The minute Lumie sees me, her eyes light up. I touch her head lightly. It's so hard to see her like this.

"That's right, girl. Here you go. A major car bed. How great is this?"

Brian lays Lumie on the towels and I put my arm around her to make sure she doesn't fall off.

Maudie drives slow like she's a hundred years old. When she pulls onto our street, Lumie's head goes up. She knows.

"We're almost home. This is our street. Good girl. Everyone is here to say hi."

Brian lifts Lumie from the car and I follow behind with her crate. Mr. Burbank gives a salute on the porch. Bunster makes thumping noises.

Lu Lu and Miss Nyla are in the hall for a gentle hello. Jordan stands next to them.

A big banner—WELCOME HOME, LUMIE—YOU'RE A GOOD DOG—hangs above the staircase and *Lumie* is spelled right!

"You can't read," I tell Lumie, "but this is for you."

The puppy club wanted to come, but Dr. Rosario said less is more today.

Lumie is going to have to get used to a very different life for a while.

There is one thing I haven't looked at yet—Lumie's guide-dog-in-training vest. It has blood on it and a few rips. I don't want to see it, but I'm glad we have it in a bag.

There won't be toys rolling on the floor or times spent in the yard until Lumie gets better.

Yesterday, when I visited her in the vet hospital, Dr. Rosario told me, "She'll sleep a lot, but I want you to call me if you have any questions. Every dog is a little different. And Lumie is in top shape—that's a huge advantage for her recovering well."

I wrote that in my journal. I wasn't going to count on my memory for anything.

"And remember, Olive, that rest and relaxation are two of the ways our bodies heal. It's the same for animals."

I'm nodding and writing. There are so many things to remember. Here's the list:

Lumie has to not move much for the first ten days.
   (I'm not sure how that's going to work.)
Lumie will feel some pain.
Lumie will need lots more attention from me,
   which will help her be calm and not want
   to move around.
Lumie had rabies shots and is taking antibiotics,
   so those will make her more tired.
If Lumie moves a lot, she'll have to take pills
   that will quiet her.

Here's my promise:

I am not going to mess up again.
If I have to stay awake for the next ten days to
   make sure she's okay, I'm going to do it.
I will check to see if her incision gets red or
   swollen or oozes anything.
I will gently touch her stomach to see if she's
   in pain.
I must, according to Brian and Maudie and
   Christine, take care of myself so I can take care
   of her, although I might not be great at this.

One thing I'm sure of, this is going to be a long week. Lumie is panting, which isn't good. I'm supposed to make sure she stays warm but doesn't get hot. I turn a little fan on; she seems to like that. I pull a few of the blankets away and that's the right thing too.

Then this idea pops into my mind.

It's based on an ancient dog song for kids, and super-simple—"Bingo."

B-I-N-G-O is how the middle part goes.

B-I-N-G-O

B-I-N-G-O

AND BINGO WAS HIS NAME—O

The melody is easy enough for me to play on my guitar. I get my guitar, tune it, and strum a C chord. Now I sing,

There were two sisters

Wait. That's too high.

I try a G . . . C combination.

There were two sisters
Had a dog
And Lumie was her name—o

The O doesn't work, but Lumie is looking at me now. She likes this. I try the last line without the O.

> *And Lumie was her name*

(I hold the note on name.)
That's you, girl.

> *L-U-M-I-E*

Lumie moves her paw.

> *L-U-M-I-E*
> *L-U-M-I-E*
> *And Lumie was her name.*

Lumie is sniffing the air. I strum a G chord. From the bedroom I hear Maudie sing,

> *Their dog was mighty*
> *Strong and cute*

I sing with her.

And Lumie was her name.

Maudie walks into the living room. Her arm is still bandaged, and we sing as Lumie listens.

L-U-M-I-E

Lumie moves her paw again.

L-U-M-I-E
L-U-M-I-E
And Lumie was her name.

Maudie laughs and gives Lumie a treat.

L-U-M-I-E
L-U-M-I-E
L-U-M-I-E
And Lumie was her name.

One more time!

L-U-M-I-E
L-U-M-I-E
L-U-M-I-E

Lumie is moving in the way that only means one thing. I sing quickly,

And Lumie has to pee—oh!

"On it," Maudie says, and gently lifts her out of the crate and carries her downstairs.

How Maudie does this with a bandaged arm, I'll never know.

Or maybe I do know.

Love.

38

Forward

IT'S BEEN ONE more week since Lumie came home and I'm ready to look at her guide-dog-in-training vest. I ask Mr. Burbank if he will sit with me when I take it out.

"How do you feel about blood?" I ask him.

"I'm grateful for mine," he says.

"Okay. Here we go."

I lift it out of the plastic bag. It smells kind of bad, and there's dried blood on the sides and a rip by the neck. It's hard to look at this. I'm remembering that dog's face that attacked her, the growling, people shouting. I point to the rip.

"The vest saved her," I say.

Mr. Burbank holds the vest and moves his hand over

it; he puts on his reading glasses and inspects it. "I expected worse. Actually, this is not so bad."

"It looks pretty bad to me."

"That's because you're connecting with the trauma, kid, which is understandable, but do you know who you're sitting next to?"

I look around to see if anyone else is sitting on the porch. "Uh . . . you."

"That's right. My uncle, the great Millard Burbank, was in the dry-cleaning business. He was the first cleaner to go organic in all of Pittsburgh, and he taught me everything he knew. The man was a genius at removing blood."

"Wow. How did he do it?"

Mr. Burbank raises a hand. "Family secret. Let me have the vest. I'll see what I can do."

"LUMIE . . ."

I can tell she's awake. She's seeming like she really wants to start walking around, which might not be a good idea.

"We have possible good news about your vest," I tell her. "Millard Burbank, a famous dry cleaner in another state, just happens to be Mr. Burbank's uncle, and this man knew more about removing blood than anybody. So this could be our lucky day. Or not. But let's be positive."

Lumie is stretching and pawing the door of her crate. She wants out.

I call Dr. Rosario, who says I can take Lumie out in the hall on the leash.

Maudie's not here, so I'm not sure. . . .

Lumie is pawing the door of her crate.

"Okay, but you've got to do everything I say."

I get her leash, clip it on.

"We are going slow and easy, which are not commands you've been taught."

Lumie looks at me strangely.

"Lumie, forward."

Lumie hobbles forward and looks up at me.

I find my confidence. In my heart I'm thinking—We can do this. You can do this, girl.

"Good, girl." I open the door and we head out in the hall. Mrs. Dool is in the bathroom, which is something you can usually count on. "We're going to take a short walk around the floor, girl. That's it, step out, you're doing it."

Lumie stops. She hates the cone around her neck that keeps her from itching her wound.

"Don't think about the cone, girl. Think about walking. Lumie, forward."

I don't know how to explain it, but I feel the movement in me so strong.

Now I'm wondering what Dr. Rosario meant when she said I could take her out in the hall. For how long?

What are we allowed to do?

What will hurt her?

She's looking strong to me, even though she's limping.

That's normal—right? After all that happened.

I look at her, "What do you want to do, girl?"

She shakes her head a little and walks up and down the hall.

I'm singing . . .

> *L-U-M-I-E*
> *L-U-M-I-E*
> *L-U-M-I-E*
> *And Lumie was her name.*

I swear, when I sing to her, she goes a little faster.

"I think we don't want to push it," I say.

But Lumie is focused on getting to the end of the hall.

I whisper, "And the great Lumie Hudson, the best guide dog in training in America—no—North America—wait!—possibly the whole world—makes her way to the end of the hall. What a champion! What courage! Yay!"

Lumie's tail is up as she puts her bad foot down lightly, but she's doing it.

She's doing it!

39

Stronger

THREE DAYS LATER Mr. Burbank hands me the vest. Perfectly cleaned.

I run my hand over the green fabric. "This is amazing!"

"I couldn't get that one spot out." He points to the back.

"It's under her stomach. You can't see it. And it doesn't smell!" I look at the vest—there's no rip. "How did you fix the tear?"

"That secret I'll divulge. A little clear nail polish. Fixes a lot, kid. It's seamless."

"Thank you." I give him a hug. I can't believe this. "Thank you!"

I hang the vest on the hook right by our door, where it's always been. Lumie cocks her head and looks at it.

One week later, Dr. Rosario says the cone can come off her neck and this is like freedom day for Lumie, who wants to jump for joy, but she can't yet.

"I'll jump for you." I jump. "Yay, Lumie!"

Two weeks later she is walking slowly down the stairs, although she needs a carry-up usually by Mark, our neighbor in 3B, the nice plumber, or Maudie. There is a second crate set up for her in the great room, so she can rest.

And people at the Stay Awhile have picked up the song.

Mark and Cora do harmony when they sing it.

Mrs. Dool snaps her fingers and says, "Let's swing it."

Lu Lu Pierce stands in front of the residents and conducts the singing like she's a choir director.

L-U-M-I-E

L-U-M-I-E

L-U-M-I-E

And Lumie was her name.

Mr. Burbank's voice goes low at the end.

Miss Nyla's voice goes high, so high that her sister says, "Be careful you don't break the glassware."

I'm telling you, one dog can bring people together.

Applause. Applause.

Whenever Lumie hears her song, she gets stronger. Maybe a vet would argue about that; maybe people who don't think that dogs have those kinds of feelings would tell me I'm wrong—but I'm not wrong.

And I'll tell you another thing—with everything I've got, I want Lumie to be my dog, but I'm not sure that's right.

Two exact opposite thoughts swirl in my mind.

If she gets fully better, if she can show what she's got and pass all the tests to be a guide dog despite getting attacked, she'll do what she was made to do.

If she doesn't, she can stay with us. She can be my forever dog.

Maudie is reading the *How to Raise a Terrific Teenager* book. She's on chapter ten. I look over her shoulder— she's underlined *laugh together*, so I start laughing hysterically, which is easy, even when nothing around you is funny. Maudie doesn't join in.

Big sisters can be hard to understand.

I go serious. "Are you up to having a major emotional discussion right now?"

She closes the book. I sit on the fuzzy white chair.

"Do you think that if I hadn't been tying my shoe Lumie wouldn't have been attacked?"

Maudie takes off her reading glasses and leans closer. "That attacking dog came out of nowhere, Olive. You couldn't have stopped it."

"I feel guilty about it. I should have done something." I can hardly say this. "I should have seen that Dad was really sick. I should have done something right away!"

"Whoa!" Maudie says. "How can you say that?"

"I should have made him go to the doctor earlier— if he'd gone earlier instead of later—he might be living now. I should have been paying better attention!"

Now Maudie stands up and her height speaks. "You're telling me that you, who were eleven at the time Dad got cancer, who did not have medical training of any kind, should have known all that Dad needed, and because you didn't—he died."

Well . . .

"You're telling me that tying your shoe was the reason that Lumie got attacked. You're telling me that if you had not been tying your shoe for those few seconds, you, a thirteen-year-old girl, would have been able to prevent the attack. Am I hearing you right?"

Well . . .

"You know what, Olive? I know what it's like to feel that way."

"You do?"

"I did that with my mother. I said, it was all up to me. It was my fault if she had a bad day; it was my fault if anything bad happened, and bad things kept happening. I felt awful most of the time."

"But you're not like that anymore, Maudie!"

"That's because I learned that kind of thinking is a lie."

40

Certain

MAUDIE IS SLEEPING in the other room and I'm curled up in my sleeping bag next to Lumie's crate. I hear Lumie moving around.

"What do you need, girl?"

Lumie doesn't make a sound.

"Are you sick of being in your crate?" She looks at me. "If I were you, I'd want to walk in the hall. Quietly, of course, because everyone's asleep."

I open the crate and let her come out. I put on her leash and whisper, "Lumie, come."

She walks alongside me and stops to study her green vest, which is hanging on the hook. I open the door. The lights are low in the hall, but we can still see. She looks up at me.

"You're going to get past this," I tell her. She's still looking at me. "And I'm going to get past it too."

We walk.

Up and down the hall . . .

The great Lumie Hudson is making her comeback, ladies and gentlemen. I mean, look at her coat. Look at the way she holds herself. This dog is a survivor, a champion. And her raiser, Olive Hudson—this girl is getting her stuff together. This morning, she was a mess, but it's all different now! A new part is breaking through!

The stairs hardly creak as we walk down them.

Lumie studies the front door and looks back at me like she wants to walk outside. I tell her, "It's too late to do that." We walk into the kitchen. It's so quiet.

I can't believe the time: 4:47 a.m. We go outside and stand on the patio in the backyard—the best place to see the sunrise. It's not sunrise yet, just this quiet kind of change in the sky—from dark blue to having thin lines of pink and yellow. It seems like the sky divided from night to day. We watch the sunrise over the Stay Awhile patio, bringing the new day.

When you know something for certain, the next steps aren't that mysterious because it seems like the world, the sky, and all the colors on Earth open up to you.

You won't see her straining when she's ready to run.

Dr. Rosario had said that.

I take several steps backward, and use my hands to tell her, *Come.*

"Come on, girl. That's it. You're strong."

Lumie shakes her head and starts walking fast.

"Okay, we've got something going." We walk to the middle of the yard. "Let's try running." I take off her leash and throw my right hand out, which says, go for it.

This dog runs strong to the end of the fence and back to me.

"How's that feel, girl?"

Lumie runs back and forth I don't know how many times.

I laugh. "Hey, I thought you were injured."

I think she forgot. She's leaping up to play. I twirl; she races past me.

Lu Lu Pierce stands on the patio drinking coffee, and

we run over to her. Lumie sits and gets a treat.

"I'm seeing a great deal of power here," she says.

"I think she's over it," I say.

"I think you're right."

We walk through the kitchen. "My goodness!" Miss Nyla says.

We run up the stairs. Mrs. Dool heads to the bathroom and says, "You're up early."

"Yes, ma'am."

We walk into our apartment, 2B, head for the bedroom, and go right up to Maudie, who is sleeping hard. Lumie licks Maudie's hand.

Maudie opens one eye. "What's this?"

"A miracle, I think." I tell her what happened.

Maudie's out of bed. I put Lumie's breakfast down, but she doesn't want it. She trots to the door.

"She wants to walk, Maudie." I put on her leash and open the door, but Lumie won't budge. "Come on, girl."

She's not moving.

"Lumie?"

I've never seen her do this.

Lumie stares at her green guide-dog-in-training vest on the hook near the door. She wants to wear it.

Maudie says, "Lumie, come. We're walking."

Lumie won't move away from the vest.

So I take it down, let her sniff it. I put it on over her head and snap it under her tummy.

She shakes her head and pulls toward the hall.

41

Made for This

WE RACE DOWN the stairs. Excitement drips off of me. Lumie goes straight for the front door. Maudie opens it and we are on the porch. Lumie heads for the trail that she knows so well.

It's like she was never hurt.

Like she never had trauma.

It's like she woke up and all the bad memories were gone.

This is a serious trail and I'm not sure how long she can go. I decide to see how she handles a rock and she goes right around it.

"Lumie. Stop."

Instantly, she stops. There's a squirrel watching in a nearby tree. She doesn't care.

There's a Coke bottle on the trail. She doesn't stop to sniff it.

All the things we practiced—she's doing them.

Brian needs to see this.

"SHE CAN DO EVERYTHING again," I tell Brian.

"Lumie, down."

Forward.

Sit.

Come.

We go to the grocery store. She does everything I ask. She waits in line. When little kids shout, "Doggy! Doggy!" she keeps sitting. When a shopping cart turns over, she keeps sitting. When it's time to leave, she walks perfectly with me out the automatic doors.

"Good job," I say.

Brian takes her leash and walks down the street with her. "I'll be back."

He's gone for twenty-five minutes!

Finally, I see Brian and Lumie turn the corner and cross the street. Lumie's tail is high when she sees me.

She shakes her head like a little pony.

"Well," Brian says, "I suppose it shouldn't surprise me. She's just got it. She's always loved the work. The problem we have isn't how she is now or how she was before. The concern will always be, is there some trauma in her that will come out at another time?"

I don't fight that, because I understand how you have to make sure everything is as safe as you can make it for a blind person. I ask, "How do we test for that?"

"We could see how she does at the next level. There's a new group of dogs going up for further training. I think she's good enough, but she'd have to leave in two days. Are you ready for that, Olive?"

I open my mouth and not much comes out.

"I'm going to have to know in the morning," he says.

I'M NOT READY for this! What was I thinking?

I pace back and forth in our apartment. It seems so small, I can hardly breathe. It's like I'm wearing too-tight clothes and my shoes don't fit. My stomach hurts, my mouth feels dry.

Genius, Olive. You did it to yourself.

If you'd just been quiet, you could have kept her.

Maudie says, "Wow. That's not much time to decide."

I ask her what she thinks.

"I think I'm miserable. I can't imagine Lumie not here."

That's not helping.

I go outside. A huge, noisy garbage truck is picking up trash. I stand behind it and scream out all my hurt. The garbageman looks at me.

"Sorry," I say.

"I do it all the time," he says.

Who has advice for me?

Who knows what I should do?

If I don't have a dog, I'm going to feel alone.

If I don't have a dog, I'm going to forget what it's like to be loved.

If I don't have Lumie—

But it's not all about me.

Brian told me from the beginning—Lumie is not my dog.

I go back in the house, climb the stairs, say to Maudie, "I want Lumie to go to training. I want her to have the chance."

IT'S NIGHT. I can't sleep. I let Lumie out of her crate and together we sit by the big window and look out at the dark sky.

"Do you remember after you were so hurt, girl, that we walked up and down in the hall and it helped you get better? You know what? I think I was getting better too. All that time, I was getting better too."

No stars tonight. Nothing but black sky.

I hug her.

So, dogs know how we're feeling, right?

"Don't ever wonder if you can do it, Lumie. You were made to do it. And because you got hurt, you know what? I think it's made you stronger."

42

The Right Thing

THE DOG TRAINING center is one hour away, which I'm grateful for, because if it were down the road, I'd be there all the time trying to see her, which is breaking the rules.

Maudie gets quiet when she's feeling emotional—me, I can't stop talking. But I tell her, "Talk to me. I need it."

She smiles. "Oh, I just think you're brave."

"I don't know. . . ."

"Do me a favor: when you ask me to talk to you and I do, don't debate with me."

I half laugh. "Okay. I'm brave."

"Profoundly and deeply brave."

"So brave, I could be called stupid."

Maudie laughs. "Only by the cowards, Olive."

I like that.

I turn around and Lumie is looking at all the new sights leading up to her new adventure. I hold my hand out to her and she licks it.

Maudie says, "Lumie, you realize that Olive's going into eighth grade in two weeks."

"We're both going to be tested, girl."

We don't say any more. Maudie's new car doesn't bump all over the place like Dad's van; I'm not used to a car that feels this good. When Maudie got a raise last month, she bought it.

Brian said we'd get reports on how Lumie is doing.

She'll be sleeping in a kennel, which she's not used to.

There won't be any rabbits around.

I made a list of everything she likes, right down to the just-right place on her head where she loves being scratched.

Dad always said, when you have to face something hard, remember some of the other hard things you've faced.

This is not the easiest concept to get across to a dog.

Maudie pulls into the entrance to the dog training center. We drive past a statue of a guide dog.

I say, "You're going to change someone's life, Lumie. You've already completely changed mine."

We get out of the car and things just blur together. A woman named Gail meets us and she lets me walk Lumie to the back of the center, where the kennels are. I've never worked harder at trying not to cry. There are a few dogs running in a play area. Lumie will like that. But this floor is really wet.

Gail says, "Sorry about the water. Our hose is leaking." She points to the wall.

I look at Maudie and she nods to me. I walk over and examine the tap where the hose is attached and leaking.

"I think I can fix this."

Gail looks surprised.

"She can," Maudie says.

I use the pliers on the multi-tool to unscrew the hose. "I see the problem." I clean out the chunks of dirt on the rubber washer and use the pliers to twist the hose back on good and tight. No more leaking.

Lumie wags her tail. She's proud.

"Wow," Gail says. "Thank you."

I'm not sure plumbers are supposed to cry on the job—not even young ones—but I do. Maudie's crying too.

I hug Lumie, but not too long. I finally say, "Okay. You go and show them what you can do." Maudie hugs her and just says, "Good girl."

Gail takes Lumie's leash. "Thank you both for all you've done." She walks Lumie to the kennel. For just a second, Lumie looks back. I wave and Gail takes her inside.

Maudie and I walk back to the car. I lean against the trunk and more tears come. That's when Maudie hugs me with her entire self, which is really saying something.

"Ice cream?" Maudie asks.

I sniff and say, "Yes."

"Beginning now and eating it for breakfast for the next week."

"I'm in."

Through all the ice cream of the next few days, what helped the most was knowing we'd done the right thing.

She was made for this.

She'd been trained for this.

She had to try.

43

The Test

I **WAKE UP** every morning and say, "You go, Lumie!"

I picture her . . .

Walking through all the tests.

Ignoring the noises and distractions.

Missing me a little at night, but I don't want her to be sad.

The whole center has fallen in love with her—I know it!

My life feels like it shrank.

I see her everywhere. I can't turn the memories off.

How she would look up at me.

In the kitchen.

On the trail.

In town.

I see a rotisserie chicken and I want to start crying.

"You did it right," Jordan says. "That's why it hurts."

Maudie paints a rainbow across the LIVE LARGE poster.

The first report comes from the center:

> Lumie is showing great ability for the work. We do not see any signs of resistance to challenges and she is adept and eager to learn new skills. She is a delight to work with.

That's an A+ if I ever saw one!

The report goes on the refrigerator. Lu Lu Pierce says, "That's our girl!"

"Did they send pictures?" Mr. Burbank asks.

"No."

"They should send pictures," Mrs. Dool says.

Everyone misses Lumie. Bunster stands by our apartment door waiting for her to come out.

Mr. Burbank tells his rabbit, "If you had more personality, you could be king in this place." Bunster hops off.

We get another report from the training center. It's called "Concerns." There are two.

She is small for a guide dog.
Sometimes she walks too fast.

I want to write them back and say, excuse me! There are small blind people who like walking fast who need an energetic dog, right?

No one here ever had a problem with her speed!

I wake up now, saying, "You go, Lumie, but slow down a little."

Three more days until school starts. I'm trying to get all my supplies ready.

Two more days. I finish my summer reading—not one book had a dog in it.

One more day . . . my last full breath of freedom.

There's a dinner for me at the Stay Awhile. I hardly sleep that night. When it's time to walk to the bus, I can't believe how different I feel. Last year I was like a puppy.

This year, I'm officially grown.

In three of my four classes, the teachers all say, "You're in eighth grade now . . ." like we all woke up this morning not knowing that. "And it's harder," they add.

Yeah, but we're tougher.

In math we are working on estimation.

In English my teacher asks, how do you think through an idea?

My hand shoots up. "I make lists," I tell her. "It helps me think." She writes that down. No one else has an idea. So I guess we're going with the lists.

In sociology we have to choose a group to study that we find most interesting. I raise my hand. "Do they have to be humans?"

Everyone laughs. The teacher looks at me like, Are you being difficult, or are you just an interesting student?

"What nonhuman group interests you?" he asks.

"Guide dogs."

"I'll accept that."

This is a pretty good day.

How are you doing, Lumie?

I wish you could write.

I'VE BEEN IN eighth grade for three weeks when we get the news.

Lumie has passed all her tests. She will now be admitted to graduate training.

Thank you for raising this remarkable dog.

The leaves by the big oak tree start to turn glossy yellow; the tall grasses by the side of the road get browner.

A few small pumpkins grow in the backyard.

Maudie has been ringing the get-out-of-debt bell a lot and I've been shouting, "Yes!" It's amazing how much money you can save in a year.

She says, "I think we can get our own house pretty soon. How do you feel about that?"

Half of me says yes, the other half says no.

I would miss our friends at the Stay Awhile.

Ice crystals form on the plants now, and finally we get word on Lumie:

We are delighted to tell you that Lumie
has passed every test . . . with honors.

Of course she has!

She's been assigned to her new owner. We're invited to the official graduation.

They hope we can make it.

Try to keep us away!

44

Crazy

LET ME TELL you what she looks like now, standing there with Dr. Maria Lopez, her new owner, who teaches English at a college in Pennsylvania. Dr. Maria is short, which is only right, and has a lot of energy.

Seeing Lumie—well, I just lose it for a few minutes. Between me and Maudie, we've used up a pocket pack of tissues. But more than the ache I feel is the love and pride that take over as her name is called along with Dr. Maria's name.

Maudie and I are three rows from the front. Lumie turns to look at us—that beautiful knowing moment—

Yes, girl. It's me.

—and back to her job.

She walks onstage, not in a vest, in a harness, walking perfectly with Dr. Maria. She seems so different. She's older, and her chest is wider from all the work she gets pulling the harness. Her head is high, her tail is up.

She's going to be living in Pennsylvania.

We get to see Lumie and Dr. Maria for a few minutes after the graduation.

Dr. Maria keeps saying, "I can't tell you the freedom I feel with her. I don't have the words to thank you for what you've done."

That's something for an English teacher to say!

A final hug. Quietly, I sing,

L-U-M-I-E
L-U-M-I-E
L-U-M-I-E
And Lumie was her name.

She leans into me for just a second and I give her a big hug. "Always and forever," I tell her.

We watch her walk away again, but this time, she has her full assignment.

Maudie takes my hand. "She's going to ace it."

• • •

WE GET A photograph of Lumie and Dr. Maria at graduation. I make a little card and attach it to the frame:

> We dedicate all the days of raising Lumie to
> Joe Hudson, our dad, who said, "Doing a
> good job is one of life's great feelings, and
> doing a bad job never feels right."

The snow comes early, but there isn't much of it, and
it doesn't stick. I've been stopping by Brian's to help out
and get my puppy fix. Maudie has found a small house
for us, close to the Stay Awhile. We're painting our new
kitchen yellow when Maudie smiles and says, "Is it time
for us to get a dog of our own?"

I almost knock her down from jumping!

That's when the phone rings. It's Brian. I can't wait
to tell him.

"So," he says, "I'm sitting on the floor with a seven-
week-old black Lab named Newton who is visiting from
the center, and there's just something about this little
guy. I was wondering if you had any interest in being a
raiser again."

I stop breathing for a minute.

"Olive?" Brian says.

I'm standing straight as anything, shoulders back, like a soldier.

I'm nodding, but, of course, he doesn't know that. And I haven't asked Maudie.

I also forgot to breathe. I do that now.

"Can I call you back?"

I tell Maudie.

"You're kidding," she says.

We think about it.

We'd have to postpone getting our own dog.

We think about it.

For seventeen minutes.

I call Brian back and shout, "We would absolutely, totally, and completely love to! Yes!"

When I hang up, the oxygen in the room has changed.

"We're crazy people," Maudie says. "You know that?"

I totally know that.

Maudie gets on her hands and knees to puppy-proof our house. I follow behind picking up everything she misses.

We're an amazing team, Maudie and me.

And it just hits me, how you can build a whole new life with love and broken pieces.

A Note from the Author

In researching *Raising Lumie,* I discovered a community of uncommon heroes who breed, raise, and train puppies to become guide dogs for the blind. This work of fiction focuses on the little-known world of volunteer puppy raisers. The Seeing Eye and Guiding Eyes for the Blind have been generous with their time, wisdom, and resources. Thank you, friends—I could not have written this story without you.

The Seeing Eye in Morristown, New Jersey, is the oldest guide dog organization in the U.S. Their mission is to enhance the dignity and self-confidence of the blind by matching individuals with specially trained adult Seeing Eye dogs, and that mission is reinforced in every corner of their amazing facility. At the Seeing Eye, help came from many directions. I am grateful to Deborah Morrone-Colella, Director of Donor and Public Relations, who opened wide the doors with heart and inspiration. Joan Markey, Senior Manager of Instruction and Training, added many layers of understanding on what it's like to work with dogs who are the best of the best. Christine Hasenbein, tour guide and puppy raiser, captured the joy of the organization in a lively presentation to schoolchildren. Michelle Barlak, spokesperson and Public Relations Specialist, got all my questions answered and then some. And Chance, an adorable guide dog puppy in training who was eight weeks old when I held him . . . and held him . . . and held him—truthfully, I never wanted to stop holding him. To learn more about the Seeing Eye, visit their website, seeingeye.org.

My introduction to puppy raising and Guiding Eyes for the Blind came through Brian Reed of Silver Spring, Maryland. He specializes in raising, training, and vetting the puppies when they are quite small. Brian opened doors and gates for me—specifically, the gate to his backyard one cold day in January when I visited with him and a band of puppy raisers and their dogs who happily tear up his yard with gusto three times a week. Throughout the writing of the novel, Brian was my go-to voice to check on authenticity, and from him I learned about the power of young people who become raisers. Thanks to those marvelous raisers who took me into their world: Kiersten Newtoff; Martha Arthos; Lindsey Herschfeld; Alan and Carolyn Lauer; Cindy and John Beauregard; Jody McCain; and Jane Santy. I also spoke with Becky Barnes Davidson, Manager of Consumer Outreach and Graduate Support at Guiding Eyes for the Blind, who brought home to me the power of what guide dogs mean to their blind companions.

For more about Guiding Eyes for the Blind in Yorktown Heights, New York, and their wonderful community dedicated to helping people with vision loss, visit them at guidingeyes.org.

Acknowledgments
and Thanks to . . .

My daughter Jean, who understands the healing power of a warm puppy and encouraged me to write this story.

My agent, Elizabeth Bewley, at Sterling Lord Literistic, who believed from the very beginning.

Dr. Donna Gaffney, psychotherapist, author, and educator, whose insights are everywhere in *Raising Lumie*. Donna has long addressed a wide variety of experiences in the lives of children and families by counseling young people and schools in the aftermath of tragedies—9/11, Sandy Hook, and Hurricane Katrina—and working with children's literature to create bibliotherapy programs and materials. The author of *The Seasons of Grief: Helping Children Grow Through Loss*, Donna taught at Columbia University and consults for the Resilient Parenting for Bereaved Families Program at Arizona State University. It's been my honor to work with her—after 9/11 we co-led Healing Through Writing workshops for teens. Recently, we helped young people tell their stories at the Good Grief bereavement camp.

Dr. Katie Hyde, the director of Literacy Through Photography, a program based at the Center for Documentary Studies at Duke University. I first worked with Katie at the Good Grief bereavement camp. Her insights into how children tell their stories help hurting kids heal.

Good Grief, Morristown, and Princeton, New Jersey, teaches resiliency and facilitates healthy coping in the lives of more than nine hundred children each month. It is a caring, understanding, and unique environment.

Abbie Zuidema, my favorite New York artist, who taught me how artists think and respond to both the wondrous and the hurting parts of the world around them.

Barb Dwyer, my sister, who helped me understand how art can connect the generations.

Karen Baehler, my sister, who introduced me to Brian Reed and the world of puppy raisers.

Johanna, Jennifer, and Gabrielle Sheridan, who showed me how walking through grief leads to deeper love.

Nancy Houtz, my friend and one of Brooklyn's great dog experts, who told me stories about caring for retired guide dogs and how magnificent these animals are.

Deborah Revesz, guide dog puppy raiser, with whom I shared a pizza that Nancy Houtz ordered. Hearing these women talk about dogs and guide dogs and raising puppies and the emotional highs and lows—well, we should have videotaped it!

Steve Desposito, my plumber at John Hlad Plumbing and Heating, who told me that every day for a plumber is solving a puzzle—and most of what a plumber does isn't seen by others, but, despite that, you'd better make sure your work is the best you've got!

JoAnn, Laura, Rita, Bertha, Mickey, Kally, Chris, and Steve—friends who provided love, encouragement, and lots of heavy lifting.

JOAN BAUER's fourteen books have accumulated an impressive list of awards and won her a devoted following. Her honors range from the Newbery Honor Award for *Hope Was Here* to the *L.A. Times* Book Prize for *Rules of the Road*, three Christopher Awards, the Schneider Family Book Award, the Golden Kite Award, and numerous state awards. Her readers know that a Joan Bauer book will deliver an engrossing read packed with possibility and hope. Joan grew up in the Chicago area. She lives in Brooklyn with her husband and their Wheaten terrier, Max.

Visit her online at joanbauer.com.